the Cassendre decree ∞

Story, illustrations, cover design and book design by

SHERYL LYNN ROSENSTOCK MARCUS

Published by: Sheryl Lynn Rosenstock Marcus
www.sheryl.nyc / email: sheryl@sheryl.nyc

Publisher's Note: This is a work of fiction. Names, characters, places, and incidents are a product of the author's imagination. Locales and public names are sometimes used for atmospheric purposes. Any resemblance to actual people, living or dead, or to businesses, companies, events, institutions, or locales is completely coincidental.

Interior formatting for eBook by Melissa Williams Design.

the Cassendre decree / Sheryl Lynn Rosenstock Marcus. -- 1st ed.
ISBN 978-0-6928249-1-7

For my husband Ira, my mother and for my father.

Thank you my dear friend, Faith B.
for introducing me to my courage.

Believe, Just Believe.

Chapters

Chapter 1	Page 12	**1995**	It's a wrap
Chapter 2	Page 18	**1985**	Under the weather
Chapter 3	Page 22	**1995**	A long day
Chapter 4	Page 29	**1995**	The number you dialed
Chapter 5	Page 38	**1985**	Time is of the essence
Chapter 6	Page 48	**1995**	Bless this little home
Chapter 7	Page 67	**1995**	Twelve o'clock high
Chapter 8	Page 70	**1995**	Marybeth
Chapter 9	Page 80	**1985**	Know that I'm with you
Chapter 10	Page 88	**1995**	The doctor is in
Chapter 11	Page 99	**The Eversod**	HIM
Chapter 12	Page 103	**1995**	Marissa
Chapter 13	Page 117	**1995**	A downtown train
Chapter 14	Page 124	**1995**	The crowd
Chapter 15	Page 127	**1995**	The only daughter
Chapter 16	Page 134	**1985**	The night ahead
Chapter 17	Page 139	**1985**	The emergence of the pool player
Chapter 18	Page 153	**1985**	Giving Thanks
Chapter 19	Page 159	**1995**	I pray the lord

Chapters

Chapter 20   Page 162   **1995**   Timing Logic Rhythm

Chapter 21   Page 175   **1995**   Prince Charming

Chapter 22   Page 183   **Part 2 The Eversod**   The Master

Chapter 23   Page 194   **The Eversod**   Spring

Chapter 24   Page 199   **The Eversod**   Summer

Chapter 25   Page 203   **The Eversod**   Fall

Chapter 26   Page 215   **The Eversod**   Winter

Chapter 27   Page 227   **2005 Part 3**   I'm Hot

Chapter 28   Page 233   **2005**   I took my pills

Chapter 29   Page 238   **2010**   Wipe away a tear

Chapter 30   Page 245   **2010**   Mashed potatoes

Chapter 31   Page 251   **2010**   The Vagabonds Kiss

Chapter 32   Page 266   **2015**   Know that I'm with you

Chapter 33   Page 275   **2015**   The holy jester

Chapter 34   Page 283   **2015**   Thought You Were a Dancer

Chapter 35   Page 292   **2015**   The Jam

Chapter 36   Page 297   **2015**   Friday Night

Chapter 37   Page 301   **2015**   Pity in my soul

Chapter 38   Page 308   **2015**   I'm a rock star

Chapter 39   Page 325   **Now**   Is here heaven?

—————————**The Rules**

Part One
Chapter 1
1995

It's a wrap

"That's it, it's a wrap."

Michael Hamilton threw down his set of proofs onto my desk, smiled at me and walked out of my office. When Michael smiled, his face, his whole being lit up like a child's on Christmas morning. Michael was my boss, my mentor, the fairest, most honest man I had ever worked for. If he didn't like a design or layout of mine he would come right out and say "Cassidy, this sucks." He was always right.

Michael Hamilton was 42 years old, yet didn't look a day over 35. He was fit, trim, handsome, and gay. His full head of silver gray hair was sprinkled with flecks of pure black, as was his neatly trimmed beard. His jaw was strong and his eyes a deep denim blue. Michael had a lover for many years. I'd never met him; neither had anyone at the office. He liked to keep his private life private, although he was not ashamed or intimidated to admit that he was gay. I couldn't care less who Michael Hamilton slept with. He is, as I've said, fair, honest, a brilliant art director, and a good friend.

We were finishing up a newsletter that we produce for one of our clients, Bramble & Bramble, on a bi-weekly basis. I mention that because it meant that every other Thursday I worked late. Later, I should say, than everyone else. Michael and I would stay in the office till about nine o'clock finishing the B&B newsletter. It was due at the printer's Friday morning in order to meet B&B's distribution day of Monday. Working late had its compensations – free dinner and a taxi ride home courtesy of H.R. Dawson, the design firm that Michael, myself and about twenty others worked for. The twenty others fluctuated with the work flow and the need, or lack of need, for freelancers. I was full-time staff. So was Michael. Working late every other Thursday also coincided with payday, which meant that I never had to travel home on the subway with a purse, pocket, or bra full of cash.

I reached for my jacket and bag while Michael systematically began to turn off the computers, the printers, and the lights.

"That was a nice issue, Cass, clean and straightforward—Bravo!" he called to me from across the office while straightening chairs and generally tidying up. The cleaning service did not come on the Thursday nights that we worked late so that they would not disturb us. It was up to us to make sense of the mayhem before we left – not much sense, just a little.

My area was usually the messiest of all. When I am in the heat of a project, especially one with a tight deadline, I tend to crinkle my unused printouts and toss them about on the floor. I don't know whether I like the chaotic, dramatic effect it gives my office or it's a natural reaction to the frenzied pace that we must maintain in order to get the workload done.

"Thanks to you and your brilliant art direction," I said with a mock curtsy.

"Touché," he replied, laughing.

For a moment he sobered.

"It's almost Thanksgiving, you know," he said to me as he approached me with his jacket in one hand, his briefcase in the other. He had with him a light leather jacket. The weather had been unseasonably warm this past month in New York. It was as though Indian summer did not want to leave, instead clinging tenderly to late November. I could remember times in years past when the first snow had already fallen by this time, remembering clearly since my birthday fell near Thanksgiving. Everything about my birthdays were always very vivid to me, as if I'd wanted to savor the spotlight. The brass ring was mine on my birthday. Being an only child, I was sure was the reason for this need of mine to bask in the attention given to me always, but most specially on my birthday.

Michael laid down his case and jacket on the table inside my office and walked around the desk to where I was standing. He took my hand, looked deeply into my eyes.

"It's almost your birthday, too."

I looked away, my eyes darting about the room. I did not answer. He lifted my chin and looked hard into my eyes, his demanding attention.

Tenderly he said, "It'll be alright Cassidy, everything will be okay."

I smiled. "Thank you, Michael."

Not only were my birthdays vivid as a joyful splendid day belonging only to me, but they fearfully reminded me of that one special Thanksgiving. Special because it marked the day that I got sick. Seven days from now would be ten years exactly, that I got sick. Ten years of worrying if, please God no, would it happen again?

I remember it as if it were yesterday. I was seventeen, already having finished a year and a half of college. It was the beginning of Thanksgiving weekend.

Chapter 2
1985
Under the weather

Thoughts were coming rapidly. Too many to focus.

BUZZ! I turned over groggily, toying with a dream of faces and train stations and zebras, surprised to find myself in my bed. I could clearly hear my mother and father in the dining room fighting about light bulbs. I turned over, ignoring the incessant buzz of the alarm clock, trying to recapture the dream. Realizing that ignoring the alarm was not going to make it stop, I reluctantly threw back the covers and stumbled out of bed.

Stretching, yawning. Great, four days off from school. I turned on the TV and climbed back into bed.

Loud. Fast.

Thoughts were coming rapidly. Too many to focus.

Something was off. Something was strange. Something was wrong. Dizzy almost, frantic suddenly. Sirens. I turned to the television and caught a glimpse of an ambulance racing towards an emergency.

Flash—

Red—

A face, That Face. The face in my dreams. A man. A gaunt smile. Dark, dark long hair, dark eyes. A sensual grin.

Thoughts were coming rapidly. Too many to focus.

I tore my eyes away from the television. My heart beating

wildly. Scanning the room, desperately searching for something safe to hold on to. My eyes fell upon the window. Looking out, I saw the familiar sight of the building across the way. That old rooftop. Next to it my elementary school. I closed my eyes. Afraid. What had happened? My heart slowed, I breathed deeply, shaking.

"What is the matter with me?" I said to myself with a shudder. Sitting in my bed, clutching my blankets. I sat there for what seemed to be hours.

Afraid to move and eventually afraid not to move, I got up and emerged from my bedroom. Mom, dad, loving to debate, to argue. If not the light bulbs then the movies, if not the government then the neighbors. Battle was their means of communication with a deep love underlying. I understood this, but nonetheless it was unnerving at times.

"Cassidy, don't you think we should have subtle light in the dining room, 75-watt bulbs not 100-watt bulbs? Your father wants 100, always wants lots of light he does so he can read his books. This man loves to read his books. Cassidy, are you listening to me —"

"Alright Sylvia, that's enough. What do you want, the kid to go blind? A house needs to be bright so you can see, right Cassidy?" He turned to me.

"You don't want to wear glasses the rest of your life like your mother and me, do you Cassidy...Cassidy?"

I stood there still dazed from the strange episode in my bedroom.

"Uh, yeah Dad. Right."

"Are you okay, pussycat? You look a little under the weather."

I pulled my hair back from my eyes and said to my father, "Sure Dad, I'll be okay. I just woke up, that's all, I'm fine."

Chapter 3
1995

A long day

"Cassidy, hey are you with me?"

"Michael, sorry. Yeah, I'm fine."

"Looking a little lost there, kid, let's get going, it's nine fifteen, you have a cat waiting for you at home and I have a late dinner appointment."

He picked up his jacket from the table, turned off the light, and grabbed his briefcase.

"C'mon, I'll put you in a cab first."

I took my coat, my purse, and the wind-up mouse that I had bought for Leo, my cat, at lunchtime. Leo was nine months old. He had been neutered the month before, but still behaved like Turbo Cat. He would race around my studio apartment as if the devil were chasing him. So much for the myth of a cat mellowing after The Operation.

We were lucky that night, it took only a few tries for Michael to hail a cab for me that was willing to go to Brooklyn. A myth was that taxis had to go anywhere you told them to. More often than not a driver would refuse to take me out to Bay Ridge. They would say no vehemently, pull off, not really giving a damn if you took their ID number and reported them or not. In New York City the myth was that you were supposed to write their cabbie number down, scream to them as they pulled away that you were going to report them and then actually tell someone.

But tell who? Tell their parents what pricks they had raised? Tell the fat bureaucrats at the Taxi and Limousine Commission that their drivers were NOT FOLLOWING THE RULES? And how? Did you just mail in a postcard or maybe waste you lunch hour downtown looking for someone to listen? No, no one ever reported a taxi driver for refusing a fare.

I stepped into the gutter and opened the cab door.

"Michael, I want you to know—I'm fine—really."

He took my elbow and gingerly helped me into the car.

"I know you're fine, Cass, you have to be, I need you."

He squeezed my arm, slammed the door and waved as the taxi took off into the late evening traffic.

"Ninety-fifth and Fort Hamilton please, take the tunnel and take the Belt."

I collapsed into the back seat.

Tired yet satisfied with what I had accomplished that day, I stared out the window watching Manhattan slowly roll by.

"Rough day?" the cabbie asked.

"Very rough," I answered, not taking my eyes off the city scenery. I was in no mood for talk. Usually I enjoyed getting into a conversation with the driver.

"I have been working, hard, since nine o'clock this morning."

"Don't feel too bad, lady, I've been working, hard, a lot longer than you."

His voice, it sounded vaguely familiar. I leaned forward in order to see his identifying name and photo. I could barely make out his name. E. Vincent it looked like. I did not have my glasses handy, I never did, so it was difficult to make sense of the name and picture. It looked like the plastic coating covering the ID had been burned.

I leaned back into the seat.

"Glad to be going home?" he said while reaching for his cigarettes on the dashboard, never taking his eyes off the road.

"I ain't going home for a long time." He lit his cigarette with an old silver lighter and glanced back at me. The flame from the lighter lit up his face so that I could see him clearly. His eyes. I knew them. I've seen them before, I thought. His blonde hair was mid length, greasy. His moustache unkempt and a day-old shadow was lingering on his face. Slime, I thought, evil.

He continued driving. Stop–Go–Red Light–Green Light. The taxi came to an abrupt halt. I looked out the window and saw that we had not even approached the tunnel.

"President's in town," he said.

"Lots of traffic— been like this all night. Pain in the ass if you ask me. I wish he'd just stay in Washington."

He coughed that deep raspy smokers' hack. We continued downtown in silence.

"Music?" he asked a few blocks later.

He did not wait for my reply, instead, reached to turn on the radio. AM blared loudly, startling me, surrounding us with news of the president's visit to New York. I let out a gasp of surprise. He laughed.

"Sorry lady, didn't mean to scare you."

"That's okay. I've just had a long day."

"Well, let's find you some music to relax you then, country?"

He turned the dial.

"Nah— You don't look like no country girl to me—how 'bout DIS FM?"

He flipped the knob and stopped on pulsating disco.

"Nope, wrong again, you certainly ain't no disco queen."

He spun the dial aimlessly and came to rest on Red Moon, Simple is The Sun.

"Bingo." He snapped his fingers. "Now this is you—you're a little rock-n-roller girl, 'aintcha?"

He tuned it in so that the music was clear, strong, and loud. We continued, heading toward the tunnel at an even pace.

(Cra-zies in my mind. Cra-zies are in my soul)

The fog had settled in, casting an eerie glow about the lights of the city. The fog soothed me. We were now on the West Side highway.

(I need the sun now in my mind)

Buildings to the left, the Hudson River to the right.

(I need the sun now in my mind)

The riverfront, drawing strange beings to its promenade as a mother draws an infant to her breast. Groups of men, bikers gathered round bonfires made in garbage cans. Homeless souls wandering, pulling their worldly goods behind them in shopping carts like children with red wagons. Red light—Stop—a beggar knocking on my window, his hat held out for some change. Green light—Go—slowly, traffic.

(The sun is now low in my mind)

Firecracker, flash—

Thoughts were coming rapidly. Too many to focus. Faces, dirty ragged faces screaming, arms raised up to God. People dressed in costumes from times past.

Red—

That face. That face I knew so well from my darkest dreams. Beckoning to me with an outstretched hand. My heart racing.

"Come my darling."

Flash—

My pulse shrieking.

(All I want now is the sun back in my mind)

"Come Cesssendre—" speaking to me yet I could not understand his words.

"Come Cassendre—" singing to me yet I could not comprehend his song.

His screams. His mad wailing. WHAT?

(All I want now is the sun back in my mind.)

What do you want I CANNOT UNDERSTAND—

"YOU!"

"What's that lady, you say something?"

I realized that I had cried aloud.

"Uh, no, I uh— didn't say anything."

My mind was racing. Dear God, please, not this, not again.

He turned off the radio and we rode the rest of the way home in silence.

Chapter 4
1995

The number you dialed

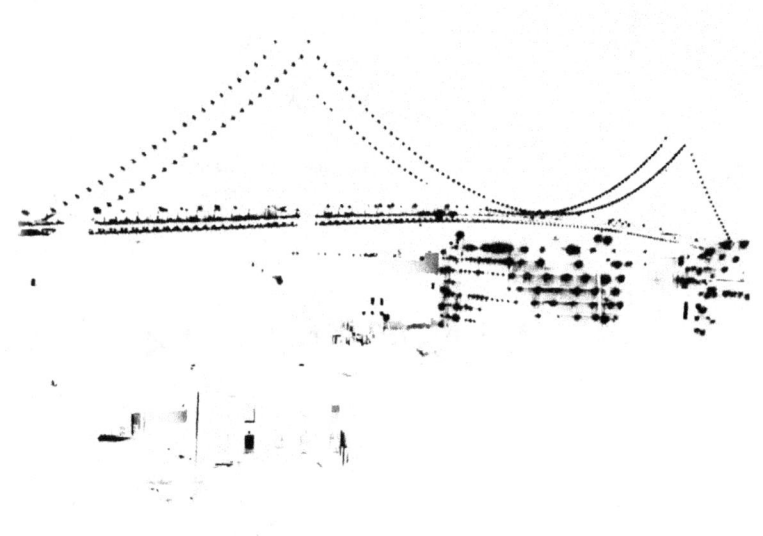

I paid the fare, making sure to get a receipt so I could be reimbursed at the office. I stepped out of the cab and stood on the curb gazing at the Verrazano Bridge, the most beautiful, to my eye. Perfectly maintained, every light white, causing the fog surrounding it to form a halo. The pearly gates of heaven it looked like. Later into the night the lights would change to red. I loved the bridge, feeling as though it were mine, looking special only for me.

I had lived in Bay Ridge for three months. Prior to that I was living in Sheepshead Bay with my boyfriend Roger. His friends called him Roger Reverb because he was a musician who loved reverb. His small first floor walk-in apartment was a block off the bay. Always, I had lived near water.

Roger's apartment had become smaller and smaller as our fights became more frequent.

The rent was behind and the bills were piling up. The fights – our relationship could not stand the strain any longer. Finally, after a particularly terrible night, I called my best friend, Amber, who put me in touch with the owner of what became my building. I packed up Leo, took our belongings, and moved.

Roger and I did not break up. We loved each other but could not live together at that time, in that apartment. He was hurt when I first moved, of course, but he came to accept it and our relationship took new, stronger roots. He knew he had left me no choice.

I loved living in Bay Ridge. Leo loved it too. He had beautiful windowsills from which to survey his new domain. My apartment faced North, which is true painter's light. I could faintly see the World Trade Center without my glasses on and Leo could clearly see the birds.

Still popular in this neighborhood was the old practice of racing birds. Coops were kept in back yards filled with homing pigeons. The birds were taken to a pre-determined spot and set free, each time taken further and further away. Together they would fly and make their way home. I could see flocks of birds blackening the sky for a moment with their formation as I walked the streets of my new neighborhood. The men who owned these birds, generally old-time Italians, would race their flocks, betting heavily on the outcome. Thousands of dollars often rested upon their wings of flight.

I crossed the street and headed up to my apartment, trying hard not to think about what had happened in the cab. Not until I was in my own home behind locked doors. Not until I was safe. I checked my coat pocket for my keys, a redundant act since I had placed them there not five minutes earlier. I opened the lobby door and went to my mailbox. Visa bill, Mastercard bill, electric bill, rent was due in two weeks. I had dug myself a deep hole with my credit cards. Whenever I found a bill waiting for me, it sent a pang of depression, like a shockwave through my bones.

I took the mail and stepped into the lobby. Always when I entered the lobby, an aroma of incense was lazily drifting about. Not strong enough to be able to tell where the origin was, just light enough to be pleasant.

I waited patiently for the elevator. It took some time to come. Mixed with the odors of incense were smells of Italian home cooking.

Bay Ridge was an ethnic mixture of people but a safe neighborhood.

The police were exceptionally keen in this section of Brooklyn, eager to cooperate with the locals and keep it a safe area. They had done such a good job, it seemed they did nothing but comb the streets writing parking tickets, not bothering to leave the task to the meter maids.

Roger had already accumulated five tickets in three short months, for parking was notoriously rough in this neck of the woods. Numerous first-rate bars and restaurants lined the blocks for miles. This was the place for barhopping and dining, thus causing the dire parking situation.

Roger drove a 1984 two-door Cougar sedan which I was systematically, yet unintentionally destroying. Unintentional, I thought, however, my mishaps with the car strangely followed the pace of our disputes.

Rear headlight, alarm, driver's side door handle; I was dismantling his baby piece by piece. The latest accident occurred after an unpleasant run-in with his and my former landlord. While backing out of the driveway I tore the right sideview mirror off. Completely.

I must admit Roger was very good, relatively calm about that as well as all the incidents, better than I had anticipated. Lesser men would have killed for their babies.

The elevator door opened. An elderly man was standing inside with a bundle of garbage in his hand. He did not get out. I didn't recognize him, but I was still relatively new to the building so there were many faces I did not know. I got in and pressed four. There was no indicator light up top, which led to a slight uncomfortable feeling of claustrophobia. It also left nothing to stare at while in the elevator. The door closed. I felt the elevator car gliding downward.

"Going down," the man said to me. He looked to be in his sixties. He was wearing dark pants, gray nubby socks, house slippers, and a stained white short sleeved undershirt. On his right forearm was a tattoo, the Navy symbol. He needed a haircut, his long gray hair tussled about the balding center of his forehead. A scraggly gray stubble of hair protruded from his chin, not enough to be a beard, but more than enough to need a shave.

We stopped at the basement level where six garbage pails stood primed and ready to receive the tenants' refuse. To the left were more pails, separated for recycling. He deposited his trash, turned, got back in the elevator and pressed six. We stood silently together for a few minutes as the car drifted upward, taking its sweet time.

"Nasty out there," he said.

"Yes, very." I replied.

"Never did like the fog. When I was in the Navy we had an old saying— 'Never set sail in the fog on the blue, 'cause like it or not, the fog'll get you'."

He found this hilariously funny. I laughed too, more to pacify him than because I saw any humor in what he had said.

Finally, we came to my floor. I stepped out of the elevator and turned toward my apartment. As the door was about to close behind me, he reached out and tapped me on the shoulder.

"Remember what I told you." He laughed again.

As he pulled his arm away his tattoo caught my eye. I had thought it was the Navy seal, but I saw, clearly now, that it was a skull and crossbones.

I walked down the hall toward my apartment. Beautiful hallway, I thought while walking down it. The carpet was maroon with trillions of white specs, new. The walls were a pleasant shade of gray and each door was painted a complementary shade to match the rug. It always pleased me to approach my home. I reached into my coat pocket for my keys and felt nothing, only gloves. My heart began to pound as I envisioned myself stuck, locked out of my apartment and needing to contact my mother. I dug deeper into my pockets, pulling out everything within. Entangled in my gloves I found my keys.

"What else can happen tonight?" I thought as I opened the door.

Leo was deliriously glad to see me, as usual, especially on a late Thursday. Whether he was happy to see me because he missed me or because he was hungry I would never know. I relished in his affection anyway. He followed me around the apartment as I hung up my coat, put away my bag and checked my answering machine.

Four messages.

I pressed the button. Beep—"Hi Cassidy, this is your mother Sylvia, call me when you come home, I want to ask you something." Beep, Thursday, seven fifteen the mechanical voice said. My mother never remembered that I worked late every other Thursday. She probably thought I was dead by now since it was nine thirty and I hadn't called her. I tried to keep close contact with my mother since my father died three years ago.

The answering machine beeped again.

"Hi this is Jimmy, the super. Just calling to say I'm running a little late, I should be to you by nine thirty." Thursday seven forty five. Beep. Beep again.

"Hi babe, where are you? I'm going to pick you up at ten o'clock, be ready, remember? We're going to Steve's? Catch you later – love you, bye. Beep. Thursday eight fifty four.

Beep again—silence, hang up. Thursday nine twenty seven.

I hated when people hung up on my machine. A flash of rage raced through my body. I furiously dialed *69, the code that automatically re-dialed the last incoming phone number.

Ring. I was going to tell whoever it was to go fuck themselves. I was irate. Ring. I was going to prank them all night long. Ring. I was going to –

"The number you have dialed cannot be activated in this manner.6425. The number you have –."

I hung up. "Ahhhhhh" – I screamed at Leo. He looked up at me with those big beautiful pussycat eyes of his and cocked his head to the side, as if to say, "What's the matter, Mommy?" He was so cute at that moment that my anger dissipated immediately. I scooped him up in my arms and sat down on the couch, holding him tightly. He began to purr. I sat there, rocking him in my arms. I started to think about what had happened earlier, on the way home. It had begun again. I couldn't believe it, didn't want to. Ten years I had spent dreading this day and here it was, almost exactly ten years and it was upon me. I would have to tell someone, call my psychiatrist Dr. Bloom. I placed Leo down next to me on the couch, got up to get the phone and dialed his number. Knowing he was not in at this time I called anyway. Ring. Ring. Ring. Ring. An answering machine picked up.

"You have reached the office of Dr. Bloom. This is Dr. Bloom and I am on vacation from November 12 through December 1. I will be back in the office Monday, December 2. In the event of an emergency please contact Dr. Kane at 212-555-3427. If you wish to leave a message—"

I hung up the phone, retrieved my date book from my bag and wrote down Dr. Kane's phone number next to Friday, November 17.

"I'll have to call tomorrow," I said to Leo. I returned to the couch, leaned back, stroking Leo gently. Why now? For so long I had been okay. Maybe I was just imagining the whole thing. I gazed out the window. Maybe I was working too hard. Maybe I could use a drink.

Chapter 5
1985

Time is of the essence

"...drink?"

"What?"

"Cassidy, I said do you want anything to eat or drink? Are you hungry? Eat something, you'll feel better, come I'll make you breakfast. Do you want eggs, or French toast, how about some oatmeal? You love oatmeal, sit I'll make it for you."

"No, ma, I'm not hungry."

"What do you mean you're not hungry, you have to eat breakfast, you're not going to run around the city all day without breakfast. You worry me Cassidy Ann, I don't think you eat right."

"She eats fine, Sylvia, leave the kid alone. She's a big girl, she knows when she's hungry and when she's not," my father chimed in.

"Thank you, dad."

"Just eat something to make your mother happy, alright, pussycat?"

"Okay, okay, I'll have eggs. Just eggs – scrambled."

My mother went into the kitchen and began preparing my breakfast.

"So Cassidy what are you planning to do today? You said you wanted to go to the city. By the way I bought a cake for your friends for Saturday, it's in the freezer – don't touch it, alright?" She beat at the eggs.

"There's a new exhibit at the BMA building," my father said, the *New York Times* propped up in front of his face. "There are paintings from the sixteenth century, various artists, here—he began quoting from the newspaper, 'a fine representation of sixteenth century masters, encompassing themes from the bible between the years 1532 and 1587. Accompanying the paintings are excerpts of gothic music from contemporary artists. A treat for the eye as well as the ear, a must see.' Four stars it got, Cass, why don't you go?"

"Maybe I will."

"What about the next couple of days, do you have studying or school work to do?" my mother asked from the kitchen.

"Some school work, I have some sketches due—I think I will go to that show at the BMA building, Dad, I wanted to go into the city anyway and it sounds interesting."

"Uncle Neil's coming tomorrow for Thanksgiving dinner, did you invite Amber?"

"Yeah, I think she's coming, she'll let me know later, thanks ma—" I said as she put my breakfast down in front of me. Scrambled eggs, toast, orange juice and a cup of yogurt. "I told you I wasn't hungry."

"Just eat," my father said.

Amber was my best friend. We had known each other all or lives, literally since birth because she lived in my grandparents' building, across the street. We had shared everything in our lives, from toys to boyfriends. I would straddle her on my bed in my room on Saturday afternoons and pluck her eyebrows. I had sworn years ago that I would wait a year before starting college so that she could catch up. I was a year ahead of her in school even though she was eight months older than me for I

41

had skipped eighth grade in an accelerated program. I never did, though, wait that year for her. I was now in FIT three quarters of the way done and she was in her first year of Brooklyn College. She wanted to be a teacher. I wanted to be a fashion designer.

I was always artistic, even as a child. My mother claimed it was the wall paper. She said she had read somewhere that if you covered a child's walls with bright colors the child would be artistic. Well, the wallpaper that covered my room was big, bright, bold red and blue flowers on a white background.

I personally attributed my artistic abilities to my mother herself. She would always tell me "Go, do something, create something, here's an egg carton, go make something out of it."

I finished my breakfast, got dressed and set off for the city.

I walked the block and a half to the train station, bought my tokens and waited for the train.

I stood, staring south, the direction that the train would be coming from. Lost in thought. Lost in time—the train approached around the bend, down there. In a daze I watched the train come toward me, it seemed to be moving in slow motion, seemed to take years to reach the spot where I was standing. Woosh, time snapped back into focus, I felt a blast of air as it sped by without stopping.

"The next north bound F train will be arriving in two minutes," the voice over the loudspeaker crackled.

"What about the train that just passed?" I thought.

I turned to a woman standing near me with her young son.

"What about the train that just passed?" I asked her.

"What train?" she replied.

"That train, didn't you just see that train, it just went by and didn't even stop."

I sounded a little frantic. I think I scared her.

"I didn't see a train," she said. She grabbed her son's hand, looked at me strangely and moved further down the platform. Her son, lagging behind her, looked at me.

"Crazy lady, crazy lady," he yelled.

"Shhhhh, Bradley come here!"

They moved even further down the platform.

I knew I had seen a train go by. Maybe I was crazy. Maybe I was just spooked by what had happened that morning. Maybe the lady was crazy.

I heard the train approaching. The second train as far as I was concerned.

I got in and took my favorite seat, the corner, by the window, facing west. I stared out of the window thinking about the next few days. Tomorrow was Thanksgiving. Maybe I would drag Amber to the parade with me. I was having my old girlfriends over Sunday night to celebrate my birthday – Sue, Elise, Amber, Heidi, Lisa, Gayle, Alice, Stacy, Tracey, Stacey and Stacy, sounded like a song. Carvel ice cream cake – my favorite. I had grown up with these girls from the neighborhood and we were still tight friends, although everyone was going their separate ways.

I took my magazine out of my bag and began to read about hairdos and dating tips. The rest of the train ride was fast and uneventful. Uneventful because no beggars came around. Fast because I had my magazine to distract me.

Time was funny, I thought. if I didn't have a magazine with me the ride would have gone on forever. I was convinced that some days were really longer than others, like a week long instead of twenty-four hours. I believed that there was some big old timekeeper somewhere that was either slacking off or playing jokes on us mere mortals.

I got off the train at Thirty-fourth Street. The BMA Gallery was on Fifty-Fourth and I didn't feel like going directly there. I knew the city well, having accompanied my mother hundreds of times to stores and museums. Most often we went to Lacy's, the largest department store in the world. My mother loved to spend my father's money there, so I knew the store inside and out. I exited the train station and went there just to look around. The store was decorated for the holidays. Gold angels hanging, Christmas trees covered with icicles. Shiny brocade fabric draped from chandelier to chandelier. A long, deep red carpet trimmed with gold stitching welcoming one and all to the festival. Opulence, shine, wealth was everywhere. It was Christmas in New York and people were buying and giving and moving about. Hustle and bustle. Beautiful ladies dressed in medieval attire stood in the middle of the aisle with bottles of perfume ready to spray anyone who passed by and held out an arm. Pssst behind the ear, on the finger, the wrist. Thank you so much. Everyone was so polite. A great big gold carnival.

"Try our new fragrance."

"Taste our new truffle."

"Visit our new boutique."

Women in fur coats, children disrobing from their earmuffs and scarves. Vivaldi's *Four Seasons* playing as if coming from the angels themselves.

"Step this way, get your picture taken with Beth Stone..."

I followed the crowd over to a corner where they had set up a large Polaroid camera to take your picture in front of a cardboard cutout of Beth Stone. A souvenir, compliments of Lacy's.

What the hell, I got on line to get my picture taken. I loved Lacy's there was always an adventure to be found inside.

There was about fifteen people in front of me. Moms with their kids, teenage guys, young girls. I stood and waited my turn.

A few minutes passed, five minutes later I was third in line.

"You'd better hurry!"

I turned around, it felt as if someone had whispered in my ear.

"Time, time is of the essence, hurry."

I turned the other way looking for the person who was whispering in my ear. I stood there, twisting my head back and forth, looking dazed and feeling confused.

"Miss, c'mon, you're next."

The man taking the pictures was calling to me.

I walked over and stood next to Beth. Flash – he took the picture.

Flash – RED–

A voice, that voice –

"Hurry, time is of the essence, you'd better hurry."

The man handed me a card. On the front it said – Lacy's. We have a way of giving. Inside the polaroid photo I had just taken was coming alive, held by a die cut in the card. I stared at my picture; it didn't even look like me. My eyes were red from the flash. An almost evil grin took the place of my smile. My jacket collar was askew, as was the collar of the yellow blouse I was wearing. The polka dots on my shirt looked more green than black.

I stood there, in the middle of Lacy's, holding onto the picture. People knocking into me, almost pushing. All of a sudden it got warm and stuffy. Too many strangers, way too crowded.

"Hurry, time is waiting."

I folded the picture, put it in my bag and looked for the nearest way out. The Broadway entrance was closest. I ran toward it. I knew I had to hurry. Why? I didn't know. Something was going to happen, and I had to be there. Where? I didn't know that either, I just had to leave the store.

I was going to Fifty-Fourth and Madison, making my way to the BMA gallery. I felt that was where I should go.

Walking uptown, coming to a red light –crossing the other way, walking till I came to another red light, and so on. Keep moving. Zigzagging my way up and cross town. "Hurry, time is waiting."

The whisper in my ear had become one with the thunder in my heart as I quickly moved. Fifty-First Street, red light–turn right–over to Madison. Two more blocks. Green light, green light, green light, as if the Gods were with me, urging me along and preparing the way.

Finally, panting, I reached the BMA gallery. I paid the nominal fee, took my program, and stepped inside the cool, dark, elegant room. There was but one other man there.

Music drifted about. I could almost see the percussion dancing in the air. The gallery was large and round. Black carpet covered the walls with paintings hanging at even intervals. In the center stood a round pedestal. Surrounding it were benches, four of them, laid out in the formation of North, South, East and West. On the pedestal, lighted from beneath, was a four-sided, almost box-like case, about two feet tall. Panels covered with paintings of sixteenth century mortality painted in gold leaf. It was glowing, beckoning to me. I approached it and felt immediately at ease. As if whatever was urging me to get here was at peace. Satiated, I walked around the wonder, gazing at it from different angles, circling. I stepped close to it and examined it in detail. Humanity it showed, in all its forms.

The music rose.

Birth, life, death and rebirth. Layers of mankind juxtaposed upon one another.

The music fell, low, heavy bass.

Arms raised up to God. One layer intermingling with the next in perfect harmony. Perfection this was, a treasure. I felt at peace.

The music rose once again.

At one with the universe, at one with myself. I sat down on the Northern bench, closed my eyes, listening to the beautiful notes surrounding me, in a daze.

in a daze

in a daze...

Chapter 6
1995

Bless this little home

Buzzzzzzzzzzz

I jumped. The door. Leo jumped up and ran into his special area. I went to the door.

"Who's there?"

"Jimmy, the super."

I opened the door and glanced at the clock. Nine forty-five.

"Hi, I'm Jimmy, the new super." He held out his hand.

"Sorry I'm late."

"Hi, I'm Cassidy, that's okay, come in." We shook hands.

I had forgotten he was coming. I had called him the day before.

"Sorry so late, but I didn't know if it was urgent. So, what's the problem?" he asked, stepping into my apartment. Leo came out and went to his food bowl.

"Nice cat, nice paintings," he said, looking around. "You did them?"

"Yes, thank you, please don't mind the apartment, I just got home from work."

"Hey, I don't mind, if you don't mind. Did you get my message?"

He looked at me with big dark puppy dog eyes. Jimmy was adorable, young, twenty-one at the most.

"Yes, I got it , no problem. It's the window," I said, leading the way. "I opened it the other day and it made a noise."

"What kind of noise?"

"Like a big Crackkkkk, and now it won't stay up. I don't want it falling on his head." I nodded toward Leo.

"Well, let me have a look, this shouldn't take long."

He had with him two screwdrivers and a needle nose pliers. He pulled the window down and out as I stood there watching. He fiddled with the casings on the side of the window.

"Ballisters, you need new ones. I'll be right back."

He left the apartment as the phone rang.

"Hello."

"Hi baby, I'm running a little late, give me another half hour."

"Roger! I thought we discussed this."

"Hey, I'm sorry, okay, you don't have to go if you don't want to."

Silence.

"Do you want to go or not?"

"Alright, just hurry." I slammed down the phone.

That was one of the things we always fought about, his tardiness. Roger would tell me he'd pick me up at ten and then call in fifteen-minute intervals saying he was on his way, or he was running late, or his car broke down, or give him another half hour. It drove me crazy.

The door opened and Jimmy walked in with two long silver rods, ballisters, I assumed.

"OK, I'll have this fixed in no time."

He got back to work on the window.

"Do you have a flashlight?" he asked me.

"Sure." I got the flashlight and stood next to him holding it while he worked.

"So, what do you do?" he asked me.

"I'm the Graphic Design Manager for my company, a small design firm, H.R Lawson."

"In the city?"

"Yes."

"Oh yeah, sounds like a good gig, you work on a computer?"

"Yeah, I've got a beautiful new set-up, new Mac, scanner, printer, twenty-inch monitor as big as that." I nodded in the direction of the television.

"Hey, sounds like a really good gig, hold that." He handed me a screwdriver.

He continued working.

"How do you like it here? I asked him.

He took the screwdriver from my hand.

"I love it, been here three days. I used to work in Howard Beach, but in a smaller building. Move the light over here, thanks. My dad knows Harry, he's good friends with him, they race pigeons together."

"That's how I got my apartment."

"You race pigeons with Harry?"

He turned to look at me and laughed softly.

"No, my best friend's fiance's mother grew up with Harry. Did you follow that? My best friend's finance's mother?"

We both laughed.

"Did you see the flathead screwdriver?" he asked.

"No."

He looked around.

"You know what that means, don't you?" Jimmy turned around and looked me dead in the eye. "It means the devil's got it."

At that moment the television came on as if on cue.

"What?"

"It's that dammed clapper," I said.

"Clapper?"

"Yeah, you know, clap on, clap off. It gets sensitive in damp weather." He glanced down at the floor and there was the screwdriver.

"This is too weird, I got it." He picked up the screwdriver.

"That clapper would drive me crazy."

He snapped the window back in place and the TV turned off. We both turned toward the television.

"I'm sort of used to it."

"Well, the window is fine now." He started gathering his tools.

I went to my purse and took out five dollars to give him a tip.

"Thank you," I said, handing him the money.

He was walking out the door when he turned to me.

"No, no thank you, you're a doll, I wouldn't take money from you, besides, let's see, for Harry's old friends, son's finance's best friend—I'd do anything. Oh, and watch that clapper, okay, you'll scare yourself silly one day."

He laughed, waved goodbye and left.

"What an adorable guy, and what an exit," I said to Leo. He just meowed.

I went to change my clothes. Roger would be here sooner or later and would give me shit if I wasn't ready.

Jeans, turtle neck, black, my old brown cowboy boots. I fixed my hair, the front all gathered up top, one-pin-back, my mom used to call it when I was a little girl.

I found it ironic that at age twenty-seven I was wearing my hair in the same manner as when I was seven.

A touch-up of my makeup and I was ready. So where was Roger? Why did he always keep me waiting?

I went to the fridge and was about to open a beer when I remembered that I had to call doctor, what was his name?

Dr. Carey? No, Kane, tomorrow. He'd probably give me a blood test and although the alcohol in my system wouldn't make a difference, I just didn't think it was a good idea. I took out the soda instead. I was getting angrier by the moment.

I went back to the fridge, looked inside and took out the peanut butter, my all-time favorite bad-for-you-food. I took a spoon out of the drainboard.

Buzzzzz, Buzzzzz, Buzzzzz

Roger.

I buzzed him in on the intercom and put away the peanut butter.

He opened the door and walked in, kissing me hello; he knew I was pissed.

"Hi Honey, sorry I'm late, there was not one, but two accidents on the parkway. Weird, huh?" He walked into the kitchen and put out his cigarette.

"I'm sure." I said. "Well at least you saved me from peanut butter purgatory."

"Oh, no, hitting the old peanut butter, are we?"

He stood there with his hands on his hips, looking silly.

Roger was six feet tall, and when he was wearing cowboy boots, like he was now, he was even taller. He had on black jeans, faded just right, a new white Hanes T-shirt that I had picked up for him a few days ago, with a denim shirt over it. His old broken-in brown leather jacket completed the outfit.

"Like my shirt? You didn't even notice." He posed for me.

I stepped back and took a good look at Roger. His eyes were denim blue, like Michael's, but much nicer, deeper. His hair was dark from the gel he always wore. Very wavy but short. He had gotten it cut last Friday. His eyebrows were light, almost blond, his natural color. Usually clean shaven, he enjoyed experimenting with his facial hair now and then. He had a slight goatee to-night, which I liked for a change. I liked change. Sometimes he looked like a young Paul Newman, at other times he looked like Satan's son. His smile was wickedly handsome. He was thin, having been much heavier in years past. I preferred him slim.

He spoke with his hands, punctuating with gestures.

Roger was very intense about everything. He would accuse me of being too intense, but it was he who was in excess, excessive in love, in emotion, in his own brand of madness and creativity. He was romantic. He was dramatic. He was dynamic. He had the energy of ten men on a good day and only three on a bad. Yes, he was late all the time and yes, he had pipe dreams, but at least he had dreams. Some people I knew never dared to dream, but not my Roger. I felt in my bones that one day his time would come, and his dreams would come true. Despite our arguments he was mine and I loved him as much as I hated him.

"C'mon Cass, we're late already."

"That's not my fault."

I grabbed my leather jacket and checked the house for burning cigarettes. I was always afraid that somehow an errant cigarette would roll under the couch or somewhere stupid and I would come home to an inferno smelling of burnt Leo. Roger always told me that I had burned in another lifetime. I smoked, but I was trying to quit. Isn't everyone who smokes always trying to quit? Sometimes I think I just want to smoke and forget the consequences. That night I was in an 'I want to smoke' mood. I found no burning cigarettes, checked that Leo has enough food and left the house.

We waited for the elevator.

Finally, the elevator came, and we stepped inside.

"Wait, Rog—."

I held the door with my hand.

"I forgot to call my mom."

He pulled me inside. "C'mon Cass, you'll call her later."

The elevator door shut.

"Just call her from Steve's house, what's the matter with you anyway? You're very jumpy tonight."

I considered telling him what was really bothering me, then thought again. He was well aware of my "problem" and I didn't want to worry him, so I said nothing.

"Nothing's wrong, I just had a very long day, that's all, I'm fine." I smiled, a false smile.

"So, are you going to play with Steve?"

"Nice little change of conversation there Cass, smooth." He pinched my cheek.

"Yes, Cassidy Ann, I am not only going to play with Steve, we're gonna Rock with RGA. I'm serious this time. This is just what I need— new blood, wait till he hears my shit, he's gonna love it—"

He stopped talking and looked into my eyes.

"And, oh, how I love you, you're such a good girl, come here—"

He pulled me into his arms and kissed me, deeply.

"I promise Cassidy, everything will work out. I love you, I want to marry you."

We landed in the lobby and the door opened. A young couple stood there with their infant daughter and gave us a knowing smile as we disentangled from one another's arms.

"Hello folks." Roger stepped out, let me pass and held the elevator door for the family.

"C'mon."

He grabbed my hand and rushed me out of the lobby and into the night. We got outside, and I saw his car was double parked.

"Come, look, I had it washed today, check it out, look at those rims, what do you think?"

He beamed like a proud papa.

"Roger, it's beautiful. It looks great."

We circled the car.

"Can I drive?" I said.

"Cassidy—" Hands on his hips, "How can I let you drive? You're not careful. A car is not a toy. Every time I let you have the car, you destroy it. This is my CAR."

I gave him a look, a puss on my face.

"Alright, I'll make you a deal, you be a good girl—"

"I thought I was a good girl—"

"Well, you be a real good girl and I'll let you drive home, deal?" He held out his hand.

This was a game with us. We made "deals" all the time.

"Deal." I shook his hand.

He opened my door, went around and stood on his side waiting for me to open his door since I had broken the driver's side handle.

He started the car and revved it a few times.

"I also put transmission fluid in and checked the oil, she's purring like a pussycat."

We set off for Staten Island. It was still very foggy out as we got onto the parkway and then onto the bridge, my bridge.

"Can you feel the difference?" He accelerated.

"Roger, be careful." We were passing other cars. "You're speeding."

"Don't tell me how to drive miss 'I'll destroy the car if it's the last thing I do—' now tell me, can you feel the difference?"

"Yes, yes, I can feel the difference." My heart was pounding, I could envision us in an accident, going over the side of the bridge and into the water.

"Roger, please."

He slowed down.

"Alright. She just feels so good— listen to this, I want you to hear this, I found a great tape, a really good rehearsal."

He popped in the cassette.

"Listen."

His music filled the car, loud.

Ohhhhh, you're giving me the creepsssssss
It's every little thing, everything you do
Move closer to me
I could not be held responsibly
Responsible for me
But I wanna get high
Now you're moving into view
I want to sink my hooks
Want to sink them in you
I told you not to listen to your friends
I know their money's green
But they don't make sense
I wanna get high.

He was beating on the dashboard, moving about— playing his air guitar and driving. Roger had written the song, all his songs, he sang, played lead guitar and arranged the music.

We got to the toll plaza, he paid the six dollars, and stopped the tape.

"Put it back on, you were right, that was a good version."

"Nah— that was just an appetizer, here's your main course, and I want dessert later." He forwarded the tape and blew me a kiss.

"Listen to this version of *Four in the Morning*."

It's four in the morning and I'm by myself
I look for something and I see it's on the shelf
I wanted to call you 'cause I got the time
Take a look in my eyes can't you see me crying
I wanted to show you but I don't know how
I wanted to tell you somehow
It' five fifteen and I don't know where to begin
I wish you could see the kind of shape I'm in
I want to spread my wings and fly away
But I can't get away from yesterday
I wanted to show you but I don't know how
I wanted to tell you somehow
Standin' there in your underwear
You got a cup of coffee
She don't care
Everybody wants to know what I know—ohhhhhh

"Ohhhhhh," he sang along to his music, happy.

"I forgot to tell you—"

He stopped the tape—

"We're going to Baltimore next weekend to my cousin Rhonda's house, okay?"

"Sure, Rog— I thought we were going last weekend and the

weekend before that, and the week—"

"Don't give me an attitude, Cassidy."

I shut my mouth. I did not want to fight; my day had been horrible as it was.

We got off the expressway.

"He's about ten minutes from here." He took my hand, his other on the wheel.

"C'mon, let's not fight, I really do want to take you to Baltimore this weekend, I promise."

"Okay Rog."

We'll see, I thought to myself.

He tuned on the radio. A favorite artist was singing.

We both immediately began singing along and laughing. We loved this song.

"That was a goodie, folks, here at BOW FM coming to you in the PM, stay tuned for more, cause 'We Play Your Favorite Songs'," Their jingle rang out. He shut off the radio and reached for a tape.

"Yes, folks, this is Roger FM, and we're coming to you live from Staten island. It looks a bit foggy still, Cassidy, why don't you tell us what's doing out there—"

"Well, Rog," I was laughing. This was another game we played frequently.

"It's still foggy out here in Staten Island, but the traffic seems to be moving smoothly. Expect some showers later on in the evening. Now back to you in the studio."

"OK, now, this is Roger FM, where we play what we like, up next we have a personal favorite of Cassidy's."

The music started. There was a line in this song that I tried to live my life by, 'Journey is the way to go,' and I sang along, waiting for it to come. What a brilliant way to look at life, as a journey, an adventure. Something to be excited about and look forward to, yet also to prepare for.

He stopped the tape as we pulled into Steve's driveway.

He turned to me and laughed.

"Just remember, suck all the living energy out of him for our consumption, love."

I wrinkeled my nose at him.

We got out of the car. Steve was waiting in the front room for us. I could see him through the window. He got up and opened the door when he saw us coming. "Hey."

"Stevie, baby!"

They hugged. Male bonding.

"Cassidy—"

He kissed my cheek.

"Great to see you both. Here, let me take your jackets."

"I thought Susan was going to be here," I called to him.

"We didn't know you were coming, Cass, so she went out with her friends."

He came back to the front room.

"You guys want a beer, a smoke?" He made the universal sign for marijuana.

"I'll take a beer and a smoke, she'll take a beer," Roger said.

"I don't—uh—oh, never mind—yeah, Steve, I'll have a beer."

He went to get the refreshments.

"What, Cassidy, you don't want to have a beer? You don't have to—"

"No, it's just that—"

"What's the matter, honey?"

"Nothing, I'm fine, really."

All I seemed to be doing tonight was telling people that I was fine.

"OK, OK,——nice house, huh?" Roger said.

I looked around more closely. I had been here only once before for a Halloween party. I was a witch that year. Every year I was a witch. About four years ago I had actually made myself a beautiful, full length, black satin cape, lined with red. The collar even stood up. My FIT sewing classes had been good for something, after all.

The house was a one-family and in front there really was a white picket fence. It had a manicured back yard and a large garage. The walls inside showed beams of beautiful cherry wood. The front room, almost an enclosed porch, was where we were sitting.

Steve returned with three beers and a big, fat joint. The guys lit up and I drank my beer.

"So, you really ready to play, Rog?" Steve passed the joint.

"Sure am—" He inhaled deeply.

"I'm hungry, man. I can taste it I want to play out so bad. I've been rehearsing with my boys Tony and Phil, my band Rachel Got Arrested. All my originals, you know," Roger said.

He inhaled again.

"Cass?" He held out the pot to me.

"No."

"C'mon, one hit."

"No."

"C'mon, just take one hit, a little one."

I took the joint from him, had a small toke and passed it back to Steve.

I didn't usually smoke pot, but every now and then I would take one hit, a small one, to get a buzz.

I got comfortable on the couch, my head back, staring at the poem framed on the wall opposite me, titled *Bless our Little Home*. I couldn't read the rest; I didn't have my glasses and I didn't really care. It felt good just to sit and drift, relax. I didn't have to be somewhere, no one was waiting for me, tomorrow was going to be an easy day, I was slightly buzzed, a beer in my hand and my boyfriend at my side. Life was good."

"...really amazing bass player, Tony is..."

Cover design due for Tuesday. Want to get to the picture collection at the library annex...

"...heavy hand on the snare – Phil rocks it..."

Design something turquoise.

"...singer went to Vegas..."

Prepare brochure for Tucson.

"...rehearsal on Tuesday..."

...Bless this little home...

"...call Vinny tomorrow..."

...Bless this little home...

...little home...

...little home...

"OK, I will— Cassidy, you with us?"

I snapped my head around with a jolt.

"Sorry guys, I was dozing off, long day, I had a really long day."

The long day sermon. I was tired of telling people I was fine and explaining that I was stressed from my long day.

"Well, we're going to get going soon."

"Roger, we just got here!"

"What are you talking about? It's a quarter to two, we've been here for hours."

"You're kidding, I really must have dazed out, it feels like we just got here."

Father Wacky Time was having a blast tonight, at least with me, I thought. I believed that time was subjective. Nothing was perfect, why should time be?

"I think I'd better get her home," Roger said to Steve.

"I hear you, it is late, let me get your coats."

He went into the next room to retrieve our jackets and returned with them right away. We said our goodbyes, kisses, hugs, male bonding again, close the white picket fence.

I headed for the driver's side.

"Hey, what do you think you're doing?" Roger said to me.

"I'm driving home."

"No, you're not."

"Oh yes I am, we made a deal, remember?"

"Yeah, but you're out of it and it's still foggy out, worse than before."

"I am not out of it, I am fine."

Here we go again, I thought.

"I'm FINE, I'm STRAIGHT, there's NOTHING WRONG WITH ME, I had one minuscule hit and two sips of a beer two hours ago and I AM DRIVING. Now open the door!"

"Okay, okay, wait, where's my keys?"

Roger was always misplacing his keys.

He was patting his pants pockets, feeling for them.

"Look in your jacket, the inside pocket."

They were there.

"OK, got 'em."

He got in the passenger side and opened my door.

I put my seatbelt on. I fixed the seat, the mirrors and we were off.

I loved to drive. The feeling of freedom and control made me feel like I could do anything. I had never lost the thrill of being behind the wheel that a new driver gets. Maybe because I never had my own car, nor had my parents. Or maybe because I didn't get my license until I was twenty-three. Whatever the case may be, driving just turned me on.

We were on the expressway, heading toward the bridge.

"Watch that car!"

"Look, I saw the car, if I'm driving, let me drive, shut up and leave me alone and let me enjoy this, Roger!"

He shut up and began looking through his tapes.

He popped in Red Wharton The Crazies.

"Oh no, not that one!" I said.

"Why? You love this tape?"

"Well, tonight, I DON'T WANT TO HEAR THAT. Give me a cigarette."

I was screaming at him. Shit, was this day never going to end. I just wanted to get home, get in bed, and go to sleep.

"What are you getting your period or something? What's with you tonight? Oh, I get it, you didn't smoke all night so you're crabby."

"Whatever, just put something else on, okay?"

He lit a cigarette and handed it to me. I hated his brand, Marlboro, they were too strong.

"Here, you'll like this."

He put in We All Dance. He had recorded it off the CD that my friend Marybeth had loaned me. It was one of my favorite CDs. A mixture of modern, gothic, chanting and instrumental. Very primal.

We turned the bend and saw the bridge looming up directly in front of us. The fog, the music, the lights, it felt like we were entering heaven.

I drove steadily on, getting into the right lane so as to exit in on 92st Street instead of the Belt Parkway. Ten minutes later we were in front of my house. I shut the motor.

"Are you staying over?"

"No, I think you need your sleep tonight."

"OK, thanks, I love you, drive carefully and call me tomorrow at work, alright?"

He kissed me goodbye, got out, came around my side and opened the door for me.

We kissed again. I started walking into my building but turned around and called out to him.

"Roger—"

"Be safe."

He looked up at me while starting the ignition.

"Beware of setting sail in the fog on the blue, cause like it or not the fog'll get you."

I went upstairs.

Chapter 7
1995

1995 Twelve o'clock high

I entered my apartment. Leo ran up to meet me at the door, his tail twelve o'clock high.

"Hello bubbie." He weaved in between my legs, wanting to be picked up as I walked in and put my bag down. I looked at his bowl and saw that he had plenty of food which made me happy. I was sure tonight that he was glad to see me and not just hungry. I quickly pulled my bed out from the couch and threw blankets on top. I washed up, took my pills and laid down, finally. It was two forty one. Fixing the pillows, I make a mental note to call Dr. Casey?—no, Dr. Kane. Leo jumped up on the bed and we settled in for the night.

Chapter 8
1995

Marybeth

Thundering horses, racing, running wildly, clouds, the sky opening up, lightening—

"...morning, the time now six thirty. Here's the top of today's news..."

I opened my eyes. Leo was doing laps around the apartment. Woosh, fast, up on top of the couch, down around on the wooden floor, sounding like a little horse galloping, making me dream of wild stallions. I dragged myself up and hit snooze on the clock radio. It was situated across the room so I would have to get up to shut it.

"...almost Thanksgiving, and Christmas is right around the corner and on that note, we want to bring you an early Christmas song, just to get you in the mood—"

Oh, no, I thought, not Christmas music already. I got out of bed and turned off the radio alarm clock.

Today was going to be short. I'd be leaving the office by three o'clock providing that no catastrophes occurred.

I fed Leo and quickly got ready for work. Morning time was always a rush. I grabbed my things and made sure that Leo was set for the day. Food, water, toys to play with. I turned the little radio on low for him, to keep him company and left on the light in the kitchen. A final kiss to my cat and I was off.

As I waited for the elevator I thought how odd it was that I hardly ever saw anyone leaving the building on their way to work; weird, almost. What hours did these people keep?

Two blocks to the train station and ten minutes later standing on a crowded "R" train to Manhattan. People on top of one another, strangers closer than they ever hoped to be. Delays, sick passenger on the train ahead. I stood by the door, facing the black tunnels. Labyrinths, a city beneath the city. Transfer, keep moving, new train, new faces. Colors, people, flash—bright sunlight over the bridge. Canal Street, all the Asian people exit stage left. Finally, almost, West Fourth, transfer. City people dressed in black wearing masks of indifference. Last train, only need to go two stops. Empty, seats to spare. Need an abortion? How about adult braces or flowers for Aunt Tilly's Thanksgiving spread?

Twenty-third Street next stop. My stop. My start, hurry, beautiful day, sunny, still warm for late November. Cup of coffee on the corner, thank you so much. Crowded elevator, finally, my office.

I dropped into my chair with a sigh, jacket still on, bags still attached to my body. It was early and no one else was in yet. Early was good, rare though it was.

Jacket hung, purse and bag stashed in drawer.

I shut the door to my office and guiltily lit up a cigarette from the pack I had bought two days ago. Enjoying my coffee and cigarette I turned on my Mac— Killer– and sat back to wait for her to boot up.

Dr. Kane, I have to call the doctor, I thought as I looked up his phone number in my book. I punched in the number on the speaker phone, ready to pick it up when someone answered.

Crack—"Hurry up"— the words floated in the air.

What? It was still ringing, yet I thought I had heard a voice.

"Huuuuuurrrrrry UUPPP."

I grabbed the receiver.

"Hello, hello, is somebody there?"

"Hello, this is Dr. Kane, I am not available to—" I hung up.

"C'mon Manny, Hurry up!!!"

"Ahhhhh!" I jumped. My screen saver had come on. Manny running after Doodle, zig zagging across the screen.

"Coming, Doodle."

Back and forth, moving the screen and keeping it fresh.

I stared at their antics. What once seemed only charming was suddenly bizarre. Abruptly they stopped and began to run into the screen. I had never seen them do this before. Deep they went, into the screen down a faintly lit hallway. Sconces with flickering candles lined the smooth dark walls.

"C'MON MANNY!"

Doodle was getting frantic, screaming to Manny behind him.

"COMING, DOODLE!"

He, too, kept looking behind him, at me. Turning, sharp corners, they came to the mouth of a tunnel, the end of which was nowhere in sight.

I was mesmerized.

"MANNYYYYYYY!"

Doodle disappeared. Manny turned to me and held out his white gloved hand, beckoning to me. The tunnel was pulsating with light to the rhythm of my pounding heartbeat.

"C'mon, Cassidy, hurry up!"

His voice was deep, not the squeaky one I was accustomed to hearing.

"I'm waiting for you."

His face was growing larger.

"I've waited for too long. Enough is never enough."

Manny's smile was turning into a grotesque grin. His ears grew long and pointy, his nose grew long and sharp. He was changing into a caricature of an evil court jester. Bells formed on his ears, pulling them downward. A spiked collar appeared on his neck. All the while his face growing larger and wider, then taller, then filling up the entire screen.

"Come back to me, my beloved."

He gave me an evil wink and "poof" his image shattered, like a glass pane being struck with a hammer, the pieces falling gently to the bottom of the screen.

"Cass."

"WHAT!" I screamed. I looked up and saw Michael sticking his head in the door.

"Hey, what's up?" He came into my office.

"Did I scare you? You looked entranced by the boys over there." He nodded toward my computer. I turned to see Manny chasing Doodle across the screen like normal.

I looked back at him.

"Uh, yeah, you startled me."

"OK, listen can you just finish up those cover designs for the Thomas National Sales Meeting? They'll be here Monday morning expecting to see proofs. I don't know what else you have on your plate, but after I finish the rest of the Thomas layouts I'm outta here for the weekend."

"I'll make sure they're done before I leave."

"See you later, I'll leave you to your friends." Again he nodded toward my screen. He smiled, left the room and shut the door.

I grabbed the phone and dialed Dr. Kane. "Please answer." I said to myself, this time holding tightly onto the receiver. It rang twice when a woman answered the phone.

"Dr. Kane's office."

"Hi, my name is Cassidy Jacobs and I'm a patient of Dr. Bloom's. He's on vacation and on his answering machine is giving Dr. Kane's number in case of an emergency."

"Is this an emergency?"

"Yes, I mean I think it is— I'd really like to see him today if it's possible."

"Let me see, how about three thirty?"

"That's great. Where are you?"

"The office is on Eighty-second Street and Lexington. 8208 Lexington, ground floor."

"OK, I'll see you at three thirty, thank you."

I placed the phone on the receiver and wrote down the address. This is absurd, I thought. I'm talking myself into getting sick. I've been working too hard, I'm stressed out and I'm beginning to imagine things. I can't be getting sick. I won't let it happen.

Suddenly, I was angry. I lifted my head out of my hands, stood up and went to the bookcase where a small round mirror was propped up in between two stacks of books. I examined myself in the mirror.

I saw my gray streak in the front of my hair.

I saw a young woman. I did not look twenty seven. Hazel almond shaped eyes stared back at me with defiance. I pulled my hair back away from my face. Nostrils flaring, my jaw clenched I said to myself, aloud, "Not again, Cassidy, I just won't have it, keep cool, stay calm." I closed my eyes, repeating the words as an affirmation.

Someone knocked on my door. I stepped away from the mirror and composed myself.

"Come in."

"Hey, girl, what are you smoking in here?"

Marybeth walked in, all smiles and young exuberance. I ducked out my cigarette in the ashtray.

Marybeth was twenty four, but a young twenty four. She was my little buddy at the office. Assistant Layout Artist was her title. She was learning to do what I did, and it was my pleasure to teach her. Marybeth looked like she had just stepped out of an advertisement. She was Irish, and she looked it. Light blue, clear playful eyes, her hair short, one length up to her chin, a unique shade of strawberry blonde. Just enough strawberry to match the shine in her cheeks. She had an almost tomboy air about her which I was sure she would shed in the coming years. I could picture her as a beautiful, strong woman.

"Yes, I am smoking a cigarette," I answered.

"C'mon, you know that's not good for you."

She sat down on the edge of my desk.

"Hey, you want to go out tonight? There's a new band at the Metro, downtown. What's the matter, woman, you look like you need a night out. What's Roger doing tonight?"

"I don't know what he's doing."

I came around and sat in my chair.

Marybeth loved Roger and the feeling was mutual. I think she brought out the child in him.

"You know what, I think I might just need a night out. I have a doctor's appointment at three-thirty, I'll call you here afterwards, okay? And I'll try and get in touch with Roger."

"Great! Cass, you made my day." She smiled brightly.

"OK, I've got lots of work to do—"

"Gotcha—" She began walking out of my office.

"Bye." She waved from the door. "I'll wait for your call."

"See you later, shut the door, please."

She shut the door behind her.

I checked my watch, nine forty-five. I looked over at my computer. Manny and Doodle were still chasing each other.

"C'mon Manny."

"Coming, Doodle."

I reached for the mouse and immediately changed the screen saver program. I put on flowers floating downward on the screen. I could never look at Manny and Doodle in the same way.

The rest of the day dragged by. I finished the cover designs for Thomas Inc. and called my mom at noon. She chewed me out for not calling her the night before.

Two o'clock, too late to start a new project, too preoccupied with thoughts of my doctor's appointment. I decided to leave. I grabbed my jacket and my bag and stopped by Michael's office. He was nowhere to be found so I left him a note—

2:00

Finished Thomas cover Art, it's on my desk, had doctor's appointment. Have a great weekend!

– Cassidy

I left the office and decided to walk for a while since I had time to kill.

My office was on Twenty-second Street and Broadway, Chelsea, a big district for Graphic Design.

I cut over to Fifth Avenue because I liked to walk on Fifth.

Passing the shopping crowds on Twenty-third Street, I continued uptown.

I couldn't stop the thoughts running through my mind. *What was going on? Please, God, let it be stress and overwork and psychosomatic symptoms, not The Illness. Anything I could deal with, anything except becoming sick again.* My feet took over while my mind wandered.

Wandered.

Chapter 9
1985

Know that I'm with you

"You're back early." My father said to me as I came in the door. He was sitting at the kitchen table eating cornflakes with milk and reading *Time* magazine. "Did you go to the exhibit?"

"Yes." I put my jacket and keys down.

"Well, did you like it?"

"Like it? Oh, yeah, it was beautiful."

"Good."

"Where's Mom?"

"Where do you think? She went shopping, to the mall, I think."

"Oh, yeah." I went to the fridge rummaging about. Finding nothing interesting, I went to turn on the TV. I did not tell my father of the golden wonder I had seen nor of my strange ordeal in Lacy's.

I flipped the channels searching for something to watch.

Wednesday, four o'clock, nothing on. I continued flipping the channels. I turned to channel nine, there was some sort of telethon on.

The MC was speaking. He looked remarkably like my Uncle Neil, my mother's brother. I sat directly in front of the television.

"Folks, we need your support, we've only got eight hours left, this is your chance to make a difference."

"Uncle Neil." I gazed into the TV, captivated by his image.

"These children know no life other than pain and illness and they need your help."

It was Uncle Neil. He was there.

"Dad, it's Uncle Neil, look."

My father got up from the kitchen table and came over to the television, looking closely at the screen.

"Cassidy." He stared at me.

"Dad, look it's Uncle Neil." I was pointing frantically.

Uncle Neil looked dead straight into the camera and said—

"Cassidy, be quiet."

"Ahhhhhhh, did you hear that, Dad, he told me to be quiet."

My father grabbed my arm.

"Cassidy, what's the matter with you?"

I turned from him back to the TV. Uncle Neil was waving to me.

"Be good," he whispered.

"Be a good girl." He winked. The screen cut to a commercial.

"Cassidy." My father grabbed my arm again. "Are you alright?"

He sounded scared. I felt scared.

"Yeah, I'm fine."

"THAT WAS NOT YOUR UNCLE NEIL!"

I stared at my father. He looked frightened and upset. I did not like to see him this way.

"I, uh, I know, Dad."

My heart was beating like crazy. I knew I had seen Uncle Neil on the TV but this fact was obviously upsetting my father.

"I'm sorry Dad, I didn't mean to scare you, it —uh—it just looked like him, didn't it? Did you see him, it looked just like Uncle Neil, did you see him?"

"I don't know, maybe it did." He visibly eased, standing straight up.

"Yes, I guess it did look like your uncle."

"I'm going in my room." I shut off the television and Dad went back to his magazine.

I turned on the TV in my room and closed the door.

The telethon was still on. The MC no longer looked like Uncle Neil. Similar yes, but not the same image I had seen inside.

I shut off the TV and put on the radio.

Thoughts were coming rapidly, too many to focus.

Wherever you go.

Music blaring out.

Switch dial.

Talk

Music

Searching for a station, knowing I had to find the station, to tune in.

Thoughts were coming rapidly, too many to focus.

A strong voice; I made the radio louder.

I knelt down in front of the boom box, my forehead resting upon it. My ear was next to the speaker, holding it between my hands. I had to hear what he was saying.

"Sunny out today, mild for November, high in the low fifties, for tonight—CASSIDY— a bit colder, high in the mid forties—CASSIDY ANN— repeating today's top stories—CASSIDY BABY— two men shot in front of Radio City Music Hall last night—CASSIDY DON'T BE AFRAID— one died in triage— Don't be scared —" Triage, Triage—

"Cassidy, what are you doing?"

I jumped up, breathing heavily.

"Dad—"

"What's going on with you today? What, are you taking drugs

or something?" He was screaming at me.

I heard the front door open. My mother came into the house and into my room.

"Harry, what's the matter? Cassidy?"

She looked from my father to me, her coat still on, Lacy's bags in her hands.

"Your daughter is acting crazy. First, she thinks your brother Neil is on the telethon, then she comes in here and hugs the radio with it blasting in her ears."

The radio, the talk had stopped.

Where ever you go

Every seed you sow

Know that I'm with you

Louder still.

Oh Cassidy, you should be with me—

"Shut that thing off." My mother put down her bags, walked across the room and turned off the radio.

She came over to me and took me by my shoulders.

"Cassidy, what's going on? What's the matter?"

"Nothing, Ma, I thought the guy on TV looked like Uncle Neil, that's all."

"You're shaking."

"No, I'm not." I was, and I broke free of her grasp.

"I was just listening to the radio and I couldn't hear what they were saying so I got really close to it."

They were both staring at me. I stared back at them from my mother to my father and back to my mother.

"She's doing drugs."

"Harry!"

"I am not doing drugs, nothing's wrong." I smiled. "See, I'm fine, I've got school work to do."

I began taking out supplies to start some sketches.

"I'll keep the radio low, okay?"

My father walked out of the room.

"What did you buy?" I asked my mother.

She took off her coat and came over to me.

"Don't change the subject." Mom was worried.

I looked around my room. The flowers on the wall seemed to shout at me to tell her the truth. How should I tell her that ever since I woke up today I had been having very strange experiences? Not just one, or two, but this whole day. Should I tell her that I was hearing things on the radio, or maybe that I was seeing things on the TV? That I was listening to voices in my head? That while these strange episodes were going on, it seemed like it was supposed to be that way? My mother would drag me to a doctor, she would get upset, she would fight with my father, I could see it all. No, I decided, I wasn't going to say anything to her— not yet. If it got worse, if it continued, if I needed her then I would tell her, but not yet.

"Mom, really, I'm fine." I took her hand.

"If something's bothering you, will you tell me?" she asked.

"Of course I will."

"I love you, Cassidy."

"I love you too, Ma, now show me what you bought."

She began unpacking her purchases.

Three blouses she had bought. My mother liked to buy a few choices, take them home and decide which to keep and which to return. She tried them on for me. All the while I was thinking, I knew I had seen Uncle Neil on the TV.

I knew I had heard the radio speaking to me. That song, "Know That I'm With You." That song was echoing in my mind. Bouncing off the walls of my brain and coming back around for more.

Know that I'm with you.

He was. I could feel it.

Where ever you go

Every seed you sow

Know that I'm with you

All of a sudden, I felt that this strangeness, these weird happenings were not strange nor weird but a part of me, of my past, my life, my future?

Mom finished up with her blouses, still not sure what to keep, and left me alone in my room.

I sat down to do the schoolwork that was due after the Thanksgiving weekend. Absorbed in my sketches, picturing in my mind what a smart young woman would want to wear to work, I envisioned myself walking, briefcase in my hand, maybe down Fifth Avenue...

Chapter 10
1995

The doctor is in

HONNNNNKKKKKKK—

A taxi stopped short, almost hitting a bike messenger.

Thirty-fourth Street. A mayhem of people, tourists with cameras, lots of blondes standing around in front of the Empire State Building.

I had a job in that building years ago. As I passed the landmark, I wondered what became of the friends I knew then, friends I had lost touch with. I guess that made them acquaintances, not really friends, I thought to myself. I had worked in the two major landmark/tourist attractions in New York City. The Empire State Building and the World Trade Center.

The garment center was where I had started after FIT. It took three or four jobs in the rag trade to make me realize how much I hated the work as well as the whole lousy industry. Luckily, I landed a job where I needed to learn the Mac computer. Soon after that I fell into publishing and discovered my true love—graphic design.

I loved the logic of graphic design. The total thought process that went into creating a page, an ad, a layout. I loved the finality of it. I designed a piece, put it together, had it printed, and it was finished, done.

It would not come back to haunt me.

My art school training had helped me develop an "eye," a feel for what font meshed with what color flowed with which layout to build a beautiful finished piece that was tangible. I could hold it, I could feel it, it existed. I considered myself damn fortunate that I loved my choice of career.

It felt good just to be outside and walking. The afternoon was bright, a kind day. Thoughts of what I was going to tell this new doctor circled my mind. Where should I begin? Playing tug of war with this dilemma were thought of Roger. He hadn't called today, but that was more typical than not. I had told Marybeth I would go out with her later and I intended to keep my word.

At Forty-second Street I cut over to Grand Central Station to catch an uptown train. It was two forty-five. I would never make it on time if I continued walking.

Bums, beggars, homeless people, businessmen, and women rushing, calling it a day, a week, attempting to make it home early for the weekend.

I caught a six train and made it to the Eighty-sixth Street stop with enough time to spare to take the rest of the walk leisurely.

The doctor's office was at 8208 Lexington Avenue, attached to an old apartment building, beautifully kept. A doorman was at his post complete with uniformed coat and hat. He nodded to me as I passed him and rang the bell for Dr. Kane. The receptionist buzzed me in.

I entered the street door and a second buzz admitted me into the office.

A young girl sat at the front desk. Her appearance did not match the voice I had spoken to on the phone. She was very pretty, with long dark hair, silky straight and big beautiful Asian eyes. Her hands were petite.

"Hi, Cassidy Jacobs, I have a three-thirty appointment with

Dr. Kane," I said.

"Okay." She glanced at the clock on the wall. I followed her gaze. It was three -twenty.

"I guess I'm a little early."

"No problem, just have a seat, the doctor will be with you shortly." She had a pretty smile.

She went about her business as I entered the waiting area and took off my jacket. I put my jacket and bag on the chair next to me and sat facing her. Two paintings hung on the wall to my right, framed images, each a graphically abstract rendition of a cat. Willy it said under one, Molly under the other. Pretty unusual for a psychiatrist's office I thought. The office was almost strange looking. It was apparent that great care had been taken in the decoration to make it professional, yet warm and inviting. Six matching chairs were spread about the room in groups of two. Comfortable, rich colors ran through the fabric and over the large, rounded, beautifully carved wooden arm rests that looked almost royal. On the wall to my left was an old piece of parchment, frayed at the edges and framed in gold. A map of the world was painted on it in a flowing, loose style. So old it looked as if it would crumble if touched by human hands. It was held lovingly by the beveled glass.

I got up to take a closer look; intricate patterns filled the outlined areas of land. The patterns were painted with small brush strokes in a pale silver tone. I suddenly had a flash of deja vu. I turned to the receptionist just as she turned toward me to say the doctor was ready to see me.

I gathered my belongings.

"Last door at the end of the hall," she said.

"Thank you," I replied.

I walked down the hallway, passing a large mirror.

The office at the end had bright light seeping out of the bottom of the doorway. I opened the door.

Dr. Kane rose from his chair to greet me.

The room was dimly lit. I wondered if he had just turned down the lights. Two large chairs stood facing the desk, his chair pushed back. A computer glowed brightly.

"So nice to meet you," he said.

Dr. Kane looked to be in his early forties. His full head of blonde hair was sprinkled with gray and came to a widow's peak in the front. A small beard covered the bottom of his chin. His eyes were dark, almost black, hard for me to read. His lashes were lush and full. He was tall, like Roger, and slim, looking like he worked out regularly. Dr. Kane was very handsome. He was wearing black jeans and his tweed sports jacket fit like a glove.

He took my right hand in both of his.

"Dr. Bloom had mentioned your case to me."

He had a majestic air about him, yet at the same time I sensed an almost sinister man lurking beneath.

"Please sit down." He motioned toward the chair opposite him.

I put my jacket and bag on a small table, sat down and composed myself.

"Well, since you're familiar with my case—do I need to tell you my background?" I asked.

"Please, tell me, Dr. Bloom had only mentioned you, he did not go into specifics."

He spoke with a slightly formal tone, although the words he used were friendly.

"I almost don't know where to begin. Ten years ago I got sick, I mean I had an episode. I was seventeen, and strange things started happening. I felt funny, time seemed funny, I thought I heard things on the radio and TV. My mother took me to a few doctors and eventually I stuck with Dr. Bloom."

"How many episodes have you had?" he asked.

"One."

"And you said that was ten years ago?"

"Yes." He leaned over and took out a file. "I see you're on meds. What seems to be the problem?"

"Well, I don't know, now it almost seems silly that I ran to a doctor, but yesterday, on my way home in a taxi, the radio, it sounded funny, that's what really made me want to see Dr. Bloom, then today, my screen saver, you know, on my computer, it sort of scared me—"

"Have you been hearing voices?"

"Not exactly, well, no, not really—"

I looked around, searching for the right words. I looked him in the eye, his eyes, they were so deep. I felt as though I were falling into them, diving into an empty bottomless pool.

He stroked his beard.

I felt too shy to tell him my innermost thoughts.

"I've just felt funny yesterday and earlier today. I guess maybe I should have waited till Dr. Bloom got back from vacation," I said.

"Let me just ask you a few questions, okay?"

"Okay."

"Have you been taking your medication?"

"Yes."

"Have you been drinking or doing drugs?"

"No."

"Are you sleeping well?"

"Yes."

"Diaherra?"

"No."

"Overworking?"

"Yes, I've been working very hard lately, long hours."

"Now, tell me—" He looked dead into my eyes. I leaned close and stared at his. He changed, he took on a sensual aura. As if he had put on a new jacket that fit even better. I felt myself attracted to him.

"Do you really feel you are getting sick?"

I thought for a moment.

"No." I replied. I couldn't tear my eyes away from his.

"Are your thoughts coming rapidly?"

I felt hypnotized.

"Are you able to focus?"

My heart was pounding, yet I could not speak, could not move. Focus... I was concentrating on his eyes, his eyes were all I could see. We sat there for days it seemed. Abruptly, he got up.

"I'm going to give you a blood test."

He stood up and walked over to a closet behind where I was sitting.

"So until Dr. Bloom gets back the most I can do is to check your blood levels."

He approached me with a needle, a rubber tube, a bottle of alcohol, a cotton puff, and a band-aid.

"Can I have your arm?"

He laid out the supplies on his desk and began rolling up his sleeves. I turned up the sleeve on my right arm. He smiled, the needle in his hand. He took my arm. His hands felt warm to the touch. He tied the rubber tube tightly around my arm, looking at me all the while. I still felt that uncanny attraction to him stirring deep inside. He tapped my vein and applied the alcohol.

"Why don't you look the other way? I find it makes this easier."

I tore my eyes away from his and stared across the room. His diplomas were hanging, framed on the wall opposite. Vincent Kane, University of Chicago, Vincent Kane, New York University. I felt a slight pressure in my arm.

"Almost done, now." He said in a soft tone. He withdrew the needle, pulled off the tube and put on a band-aid. He disposed of the needle, put the kit back in the closet and sat back down.

"Cassidy, my opinion is that you're overworked and your imagination is getting the best of you."

He leaned back in his chair and crossed his legs as I pulled down my sleeve.

"Now, you said you only had one instance and that was ten years ago, correct?"

"Correct."

"The longer someone goes without an upset, the less likely it is that an episode will reoccur. I wouldn't worry, try and take it easy, definitely refrain from smoking marijuana. Your blood test results will be in by Wednesday, but Dr. Bloom won't be back till the second so why don't you come back on Wednesday and we'll see what your blood tells us."

He lifted his right eyebrow, punctuating his question.

"Alright, I will."

I got up, put on my jacket and reached for my bag. He stood up to say good bye. Again, he took my right hand with both of his.

"Very nice to meet you," I said.

"Believe me, it was my pleasure." He held my eye as well as my hand that one second too long, making me a bit uncomfortable.

I stopped in the ladies' room to freshen up before I left. He was strange, I thought as I fixed my lipstick. Nice, though, very friendly, too friendly? He had turned on his sexuality like I was now turning on the water faucet, and I wondered if he even realized.

I made an appointment for the following week, same time, with the pretty receptionist. I checked my watch and couldn't believe it said four thirty. It had felt like I was in there for ten minutes, not an hour.

I said goodbye and stepped into the street.

Vincent Kane sat forward in his chair and pressed the intercom.

"Alexandra, you may leave, now."

"Yes, sir, I will."

Alexandra put down the pen she was holding, stood up, took her coat from the closet and left the office in one fluid motion.

After Alexandra left he leaned his head back, closed his eyes and rested his fingertips under his chin.

I have seen her, Sire.

Is she beautiful?

Yes, she is beautiful.

More beautiful than before?

If it is possible, she is more beautiful.

Is she deserving of this?

Yes, I believe she is deserving.

Is she frightened?

Yes, she is beginning to be frightened.

Does she trust you?

No, Sire, I do not believe she trusts me.

Do you have the blood?

Yes, master, I have the blood.

Bring the blood to me.

Yes, Sire.

Vincent picked up the vial containing Cassidy's blood and vanished into the air.

The lights remained, glowing dimly.

Chapter 11
The Eversod

HIM

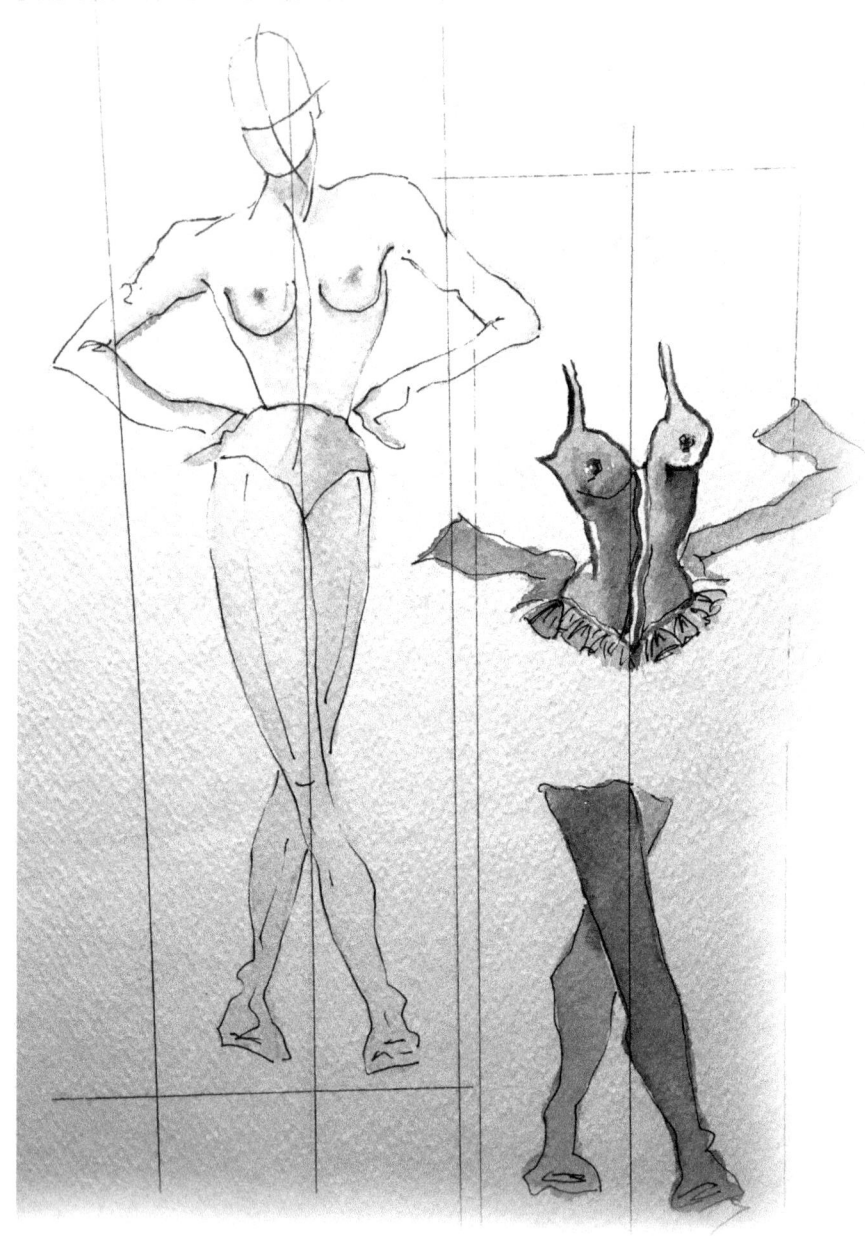

Vincent materialized in front of HIM. HE was reclined, HIS throne facing a wall of glass. Enclosed in the glass were fish with colors so bright it would have blinded the human eye. Aquamarine water flowing gently across the space. Vincent was taken aback by the decor. When he had left the chamber was brown, brown animal skins lying about, large brown throw pillows, wooden armories. Now it was modern, leather couches, bold prints on the circular granite, a graphic zebra rug, tall candles, standing in groups. Sometimes it was medieval, at others art deco, HIS whim ruled—always. HIS throne, her throne, the only constants in HIS ever-changing chamber.

HE spoke, still facing away from where Vincent stood.

"Do you have the blood?"

"Yes, sire, I have it here." Vincent held the vial firmly in his hand.

HE turned in his throne, around, slowly, to face Vincent. HE was still sitting, relaxed. HIS legs spread slightly, HIS right hand resting under his chin.

"Let me see."

Vincent held the vial out, toward HIM, the blood catching the candle light and glowing warmly.

HE stared at the scarlet fluid, HIS eyes fixed upon the vessel.

Suddenly, HE jumped up and seized the flask. HIS movements swifter than a panther's. HE gracefully stepped back and held it to the light, gazing at the red liquid lovingly.

"I can't see her–Vincent," HE whispered.

"I CANNOT SEE HER, BECAUSE OF THESE RULES, I cannot see her with my mind's eye—"

HE circled the room, pacing.

"I can remember her touch, her feel, the eagerness of her warmth, the beauty of her soul, I can remember her brilliance, her compassion, the grace in her heart. Yes, these things I can remember, of ages and centuries with her scent upon my lips, the fire in her embrace, the sweetness of her flower. I shall go mad, I can wait no longer, my suffering has festered for too many years.

It is time, TIME I SAY, damn these incessant rules—"

HE poured the blood into a crystal goblet, careful not to spill a drop, and held it in a toast.

"To my beloved, my Cassendre, my Juliet, my Cleopatra, my soulmate. I count the moments till we can be as one, again—"

HE closed his eyes, held the glass to HIS lips and slowly drank the blood.

Chapter 12
1995

Marissa

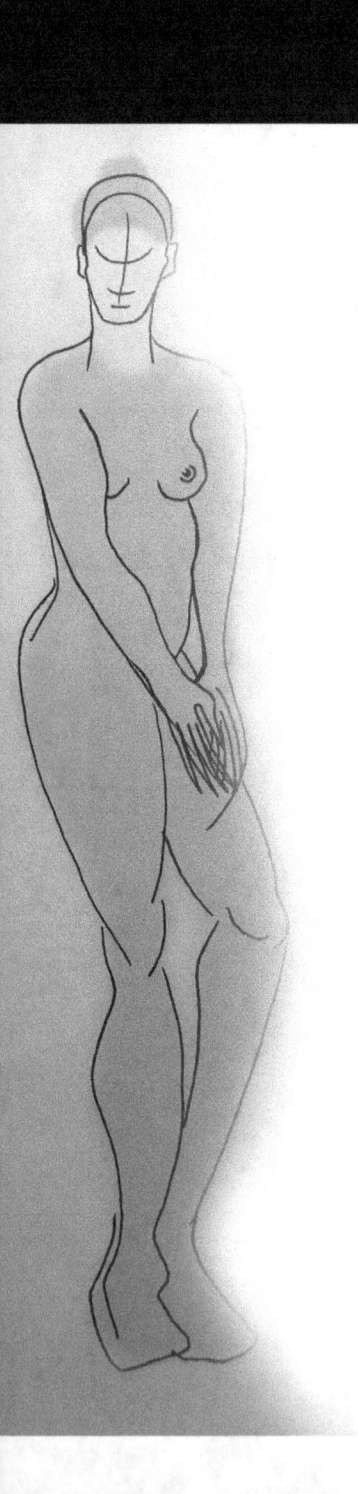

I felt somewhat better just for having seen a doctor. He was right, I was working too hard and letting my imagination run wild. Dr. Bloom had also once told me that the longer I went with being well the more I would be well. Ten years was a pretty long time. I mentally vowed never to smoke pot again. I walked to the corner searching for a phone. There were two on the other side of the street. Both were occupied by the time I crossed so I patiently waited my turn. A UPS man finished his conversation and I stepped up to dial Marybeth. She answered on the first ring.

"H.R. Dawson."

"Hi, it's me, Cassidy." I said into the dirty public phone.

"Cassidy, woman, where are you? I've been waiting for your call. I was getting worried, it's a quarter to five."

"I just got out of my doctor's appointment, I'm on the Upper East Side, what's up? Did Roger call?"

"No, no Roger, you still wanna go out?" She sounded anxious.

"I guess so, I mean, yeah, I want to go out. I'll just try and call him, he can meet up with us if he wants to. Where should I meet you? Where did you say you wanted to go again?"

"Well, I wanted to go see this new band, but I picked up the paper and guess what? There's a poetry reading at seven-thirty at The Grogle Bar in the Village. You wanted to go to one, didn't you?"

"Oh! Excellent! Yes! I'll meet you on Sixth Avenue and Eighth Street." I was excited.

"OK, I'm on my way now. I'll see you in about half an hour."

I hung up.

I had always wanted to go to a poetry reading, they were very popular lately. I took out another quarter and dialed Roger at home. His answering machine picked up, so I left him a message.

I took out yet another quarter. Time to check in with Mom.

"Hello."

"Hi, Ma, it's me."

"Cassidy, where are you?"

"I'm in the city, listen I can't talk, I'm meeting a friend and I'm going out. I just wanted to tell you I wouldn't be coming home straight from work."

"How are you getting home?"

She always asked me that.

"If I don't meet up with Roger I'll leave the city early, I gotta go, love you—"

"Cassidy, be careful, I don't like you taking the train home late by yourself."

"Don't worry, I'll be careful. I gotta go, Ma, bye."

I hung up. My bases were covered. I had called Roger, I had called my mom, now it was time to play.

I found the subway and made my way downtown. It was the heart of rush hour, people everywhere. Twenty minutes later I was standing in front of Sixth Avenue and Eighth Street waiting for Marybeth. I wasn't waiting long before I saw her coming down the block, her blue derby on her head. She apologized for being late and I told her not to be silly, the reading didn't start till seven thirty, so we stopped into a small bar along the way to kill time and get a bite to eat. The bar was crowded but we managed to find two empty stools. We each ordered a pint of draft beer and decided to share an appetizer.

"Cheers," she said.

"To what?" I asked.

"To your new painting. Didn't you tell me you had finished it?"

"Yes, I finished it the night before last, it came out great." We clinked our glasses. Music was playing loudly on the jukebox. We were almost shouting to each other.

"So what's up, Cass?" she said.

"What a week I've had, Marybeth. I've been working like a dog lately. I'm exhausted. I'm so glad it's the weekend."

"Hi, there."

I turned around; some guy behind me was greeting his friend. I had thought he was talking to me.

I turned back to Marybeth.

"Anyway, what was I saying? Oh yeah I'm so glad it's Friday, and I'm so excited we're going tonight, how nice that you remembered I wanted to go to a poetry reading. You're such a doll."

"I'm just a good listener."

She looked pleased.

"Tell me, how's it going at work, are you having much trouble with Quark?"

"Hey, miss..."

The guy from before was tapping me on the shoulder. I turned around to him.

"Yes? Hello there, my friend. Is your name Joe?"

"Yes!" he answered. We all laughed.

"Bye, Joe," I said.

"How weird," Marybeth said.

"Na, he looked liked a Joe."

We both laughed.

"Cassidy, I always told you that you were a witch, even your gray streak is coming in."

I lifted my hand to the front of my hair where a shock of gray hair grew. It had started coming in sometime after my seventeenth birthday. I always thought from the horror I had been through, but family tales said my grandfather had the same streak. I began coloring it two years prior, but keeping up with it was sometimes difficult. It grew in so fast.

Our chicken fingers came and we began to munch out, all the while gossiping about people in the office. When we were done, I excused myself and went into the ladies' room. A speaker was set up inside, so that the music was just as loud in there. There was no one else in the room.

I brushed my hair, staring into my reflection. The song that had been playing ended and there was silence for a moment.

Then THE song came on.

I knew this song like I knew the sound of my own voice.

Where ever you go

Every seed you sow

My song, my anthem. The brush dropped out of my hand and fell into the sink. I leaned on the counter top looking at myself.

Know that I'm with you

I had a choice, I knew. I could go mad. I could run back into the bar screaming and pulling at my hair, trying to escape from my own mind, or I could accept.

Accept that yes, strange things were happening to me. Yes, this damn song had followed me around for years. Yes, it could all be coincidence and fatigue.

I chose to accept.

I picked up the brush and put it away.

Oh don't you know

I love you so

I took out my lipstick and applied it. Rubbing my lips together to make it perfect. I smiled.

Every time you smile

Every time you laugh

Suddenly I found this all diabolically funny. I started laughing, throwing my head back and giving out an evil, wicked howl. No one would ever believe the mental anguish I went through. I was going to take this all with a grain of salt. Maybe Marybeth was right, maybe I was a witch.

Two young girls walked into the bathroom, seeing me laughing to myself. They gave me a strange look as I walked out, but I didn't give a damn.

I went back to Marybeth at the bar. We got our check, paid, and left. It was six forty-five, perfect timing.

We walked over to Grogles. The night was beautiful, and the Village was crowded.

We got to the bar and paid the five-dollar cover charge.

"You're just in time, the reading's just beginning," the bouncer said.

"I thought it started at seven-thirty." Marybeth replied while putting her change away.

"No, it was a misprint in the paper, what can you do?" The big man shrugged.

We stepped inside.

The place was dark. On the side of the room was a black wooden platform that acted as a stage. A single spotlight bounced off the chrome bar stool placed in the center. A man stepped up and began positioning the microphone.

Tables crowded with patrons surrounded the stage. Low flickering candles were set on each one.

We sat down, toward the front, across from each other. A waitress appeared immediately, took our beer order and just as quickly she returned with our drinks. I had to move my chair in order to see the man who began speaking.

"Ladies and gentlemen, welcome to Grogles Friday night poetry reading." There was light applause.

"We have three performers tonight and as always after the show we welcome anyone who would like to step up to the mike and perform their writings. We like to encourage the local artist community in any way we can." More applause. "Thank you, now, I'd like to introduce Marissa Ringel." Once more, applause.

I turned back around and gave the young girl my full attention.

She stepped up to the mike. She had long dark hair pulled back into a simple pony tail. She was wearing a black unitard, long sleeved, with black cotton gloves and black ballet slippers. She crouched into a fetal position. Soft music started playing in the background, an instrumental piece, mostly piano. The spotlight came on and she slowly rose to the music.

"Why are you making me leave?" she shouted, grabbing everyone's attention. The din of the audience became a distant hush.

"Forcing my hand." Her arm swept across the room.

"And holding the door open so wide that marching bands would have room to pass—"

She hugged her shoulders.

"Was I not good to you?"

She stepped out, thrusting herself forward toward the audience.

"Do you think so little of yourself that you must drag me down where the ants crawling in the yard have become my constant companions?"

Her hands held her face and she continued softly.

"What has you so frightened?

"Have the lies and the bills and the drinks become so much of a burden that you want to share in the sheer pleasure of it, my darling?"

She stepped back, hands clasped behind her, her head high.

"Why did you choose me?

"Was I an easy target,

"A willing victim,

"Fay Raye at the altar beckoning to you with my chance of salvation in one hand and my credit card in the other?"

Hands to her side, palms open.

"Why have I waited so long to leave?

"Did I feel that maybe I was not good enough to warrant some downright decent behavior?

"That some adolescent act had put me in contention for everlasting purgatory?"

Again she held herself, standing to the side, squinting into the smoke filled spotlight.

"Why am I leaving now?

"I have finally come into myself

"Stepped gingerly into Cinderella's slipper and damn—"

She released her hold on herself and stood with her hands

joined in front of her, almost shaking.
"It fits so well
Prince Charming just might be on that next uptown train after all."
The music faded.
The spotlight died out and loud clapping filled the room.
The spotlight came back on, piercing the darkness. She smiled and began speaking in a conversational tone. Just standing there and holding the mike. Everyone quieted.
"He left me alone so much
I began to like it
He told me I was ugly so often
I began to believe it
He took his failings, his insecurities
His fears and projected them on to me
Like a spotlight gently caressing the curves of a starlet
Standing alone on a stage."

She looked out into the audience and her eyes locked with mine.

"Whatever monster had invaded his being
Was knocking on my kitchen door
Demanding to be let in, nurtured,
Played with and adored
Whatever downright nastiness that was
Rattling inside his bones
Was slowly seeping into mine
Settling into the bright corners of my soul
And tainting them with the stain of anger
A dark ugly color."

She held my gaze. I was almost uncomfortable.

"Whatever demon that was festering within
Was turning his blue eyes to black
The evil, standing behind and painting
With a broad, firm confident stroke."

Her head dropped to her chin. The spotlight cut out and I felt
released. Loud applause once more rang out for her. She was good.
　Again, the spotlight came on.
　She started moving side to side, rocking, her arms snaking in
a fluid motion.

"What birds of a feather dare
Flock together there
Deep in your innermost thoughts."

She was moving to the rhythm of her poem.

"What motivating factor
Has filled you with laughter
While chasing the madman with warts
How deep does your river flow
Observing your childhood go
Off where the adults roam free
How far can you hit the ball
Up on stage standing tall
Singing your heart out for me
How fast can your auto drive
Racing flying

So alive
Car and body molded as if one
What kind of man lies inside
Despite the fact we must divide
Time will tell once the deed is done."

She stopped moving, staring straight ahead.

"Conventionality is not your forte
9 to 5's just not your size
Responsibility— That's for suckers
Don't shed a tear for we who cry."

The spotlight faded out, ending with a halo surrounding her face. Applause filled the room. She bowed, indicating the end of her performance.

This girl was excellent, I thought. She had touched something deep inside of me. The other two acts, although they were longer, went by in a blur for my thoughts were preoccupied with Marissa Ringel's performance. Afterwards three amateurs got up, and I gave them credit for having the balls to get up and read their poems to the crowd.

It was eight thirty when we ordered our last round of drinks. I wanted to be on the train by nine-fifteen. Any later than that would be too late for me and I would be uneasy to travel on the subway by myself.

The bar area was filling with people as we finished up and got ready to go. Signaling for the check, I sat back, jacket on, ready to leave.

"Michael seems so happy these days," Marybeth said, draining her glass of the last drop of beer.

"I know, I've noticed also. I'm glad, I think it's his new apartment, he finally feels settled. He's a dynamite person, best boss I ever had."

"Me too," she said.

"I think the difference is that he really cares. I mean, about everything, the work, the people under him. He's more of a friend to me than a boss. I feel like if I ever really needed him, I could turn to him and he'd be there, you know what I mean?"

"I know exactly what you mean. I've only been working for him nine months and I feel it, you've been with him for what—four years?"

The waitress returned with our check, cutting off our conversation. We got up and left a tip on the table. We had to pass through the bar to get to the front door. it was a tight squeeze. I was leading the way when a hand held onto my sleeve as I passed through the crowd. I turned to see who was holding me back.

"I know you," she said, pointing at me with her finger while holding onto her drink.

"I've seen you before."

It was her, Marissa Ringel.

"Hi, I don't know you, but I just saw your act, you were great, really good," I said to her. Her hair was loose now, out of the ponytail and looking wild. She still had on her unitard but her hands were bare. Clearly, she was the center of attention amidst a small crowd of people, an "artsy" looking group.

"I know her, I know her." She was getting loud, clutching at her companions and pointing to me.

Was this chick on drugs, I wondered? I continued walking.

Marybeth was right behind me.

"Is there a problem, Cass?"

Marybeth would have killed for me.

Marissa Ringel stepped forward, pushing off her friends who were trying to hold her back. She looked straight into my eyes—

"Go back, go back where you came from, HE'S waiting."

"C'mon Cassidy." Marybeth was gently pushing me from behind. "Let's go."

Marissa let me pass. We left the bar and made it to the street.

"That's New York for you. I would have sworn that girl was on acid, probably why she was so out there on stage. She was tripping. Cass, are you okay? You look a little nervous, girl." Marybeth started laughing.

"You should have seen your face when she started saying 'Go back, Go back where you came from, HE'S waiting'."

Marybeth was running circles around me, carrying on.

"HE'S waiting."

She was shouting and laughing, people were looking at us. I started laughing too.

"What a nut job, Cass she was crazy. Oh! your gray is bigger, bigger than before! Did she scare you that much?"

I touched my hair. Inside I knew, I was not afraid of Marissa, I knew HE was waiting.

"C'mon, I've got to go, it's getting late," I said, checking my watch.

"Okay, okay." She was still laughing.

"Go back," she whispered. "HE'S waiting."

Marybeth walked me to the West Fourth Street train station, we said our goodbyes and I descended into the New York City Subway system. More like descending into hell.

Chapter 13
1995

A downtown train

The sound of loud steel drums filled the station as I waited for a downtown train. I was waiting for a D or a B or a Q. Anything that came first. My goal was to keep moving for I had at least two, maybe three trains to go till I got home, depending on the connections I made. I stood there, in the center of the platform, where the conductor stands on the train as my father had taught me, aware of everyone near or approaching. The slight daze from the few drinks I had consumed earlier had totally dissipated with the need for me to be ready for anything. After all, it was Friday night and I was a young woman, alone, in a potentially dangerous situation — riding the New York City Subway.

Twenty feet from where I was standing a Rastafarian broke into a rendition of "Silent Night" on the steel drums reminding me of the fast approaching holiday season.

Finally, a D train pulled in and I got on, taking my favorite seat by the window. I checked my watch, nine fifteen, I was right on schedule.

The car was nearly empty. Most of the passengers had disembarked at West Fourth, where I had gotten on.

Broadway Lafayette, Canal Street, the train plodded on at a steady pace as we began crossing the Manhattan Bridge.

I loved to see the beautiful nighttime view of the Southern tip of Manhattan, the World Trade Center glowing like two birth-day candles.

The train stopped with a jolt in the middle of the bridge. "De-lays ahead," the conductor announced.

Through the doors at the end of the car a beggar appeared, limping his way down the aisle. His clothes were ragged, and his skin had a sickly yellow pallor to it. He looked like he hadn't bathed in weeks and as he approached me, the stench surround-ing him confirmed it. He stopped in the middle of the aisle.

"Ladies and gentlemen, my name is Raphael. You may have heard of my namesake, St. Raphael, the patron saint of trav-elers. I find myself traveling through life in this dire situation through no fault of my own. My home was destroyed in a fire and I fell upon hard times and I pray to St. Raphael that you yourselves never find yourselves in my position. I beg of you, ladies and gentlemen, out of the kindness of your hearts, if you could spare some change, anything, a nickel, a penny, maybe even some food, anything, I will pray to God almighty for your salvation. Thank you for listening."

He walked directly over to me and held out a dirty old paper coffee cup. I reached into my jacket pocket and felt some change inside. I took it all out and held it out toward his cup, looking up at him. He looked directly at me with a clear, intense stare. *He's lying*, I thought instantly. I didn't know where the thought came from or what brought it on.

The train jerked back into motion and I dropped the change into his cup.

"Thank you kindly, Miss, I thank you, and HE thanks you."

He held my eye another heartbeat longer and shuffled off to the man sitting behind me. After we crossed the bridge, I waited at DeKalb Avenue for my next train, an N or an R. It wasn't long before a semi-crowded N pulled up. A late Wall Street crowd was scattered about the car looking tired and relaxed. I took my place among them and settled in for the bulk of my ride. I leaned my head back, clutching my bag to my body and fell into the same weary semi-conscious state that the other passengers were in. Finding my eyes wanting to close, I snapped my head, trying to stay awake. The harder I tried to keep my eyes open, the closer I came to falling asleep. Finally, the motion of the train took over the battle and I fell out. Utter blackness, for a moment, it seemed.

Eyes open, wide awake, heart pounding. What train was this? What stop was this? Shit, what day was this? I looked around the car.

Shit, where did everyone go?

Trains flying,

Big Yellow N.

Lovely voice over the loudspeaker.

Shit— missed my stop.

Pacing through the car.

Tunnels flying by.

When will this train stop—

I want to get off—

OK, ready? 1-2-3-Rationalize—

Cass, calm down, take it easy—

"Eighth Avenue will be the next stop."

Lovely, lovely voice.

Cass don't bug out, just take it easy.

Station in sight, dark outside station. I just have to go around to the other side and take the train in the opposite direction one stop to get my local train. It's only one stop, it's only one stop.

The doors opened and deposited me onto the deserted outside platform. The wind was picking up, and it was cold. I walked quickly to the south end where the stairs were, my heels echoing against the concrete slab.

I should take a cab home.

I don't have enough cash.

I should take one anyway and stop at a bank.

OK, Cass, ready? 1-2-3 Rationalize. Cassidy, just get over to the other side, a train will be coming any minute and you just have to go back one stop for the local R home.

Click, click.

Click, click.

My heels, tapping out a tune. I raced up the staircase, around and down to the other side. Still I had not seen a person.

Was that good or bad?

Get to the center of the platform where the conductor stands.

The wind, whipping my hair up and around and bending the trees as if in submission. The shadows from the remaining few leaves dancing beneath my feet.

To the left, a stairwell, leading down to an empty platform. How strange, black wire fencing enclosing the entrance, the only entrance. Movement below. Music drifting upward, Mozart, "Concerto #21."

Bending closer, grasping onto the fence. A hint of gliding figures dancing to the music, a rustle of fabric.

The train exploded into the station, startling me out of my reverie. I stood up and got on.

A man sat, fast asleep. I moved quickly away from him,

spooked, and stood by the doorway, looking out at the tracks opposite, speeding by, waiting for my stop. My reflection, a ghostly image against the trees lining the railway. I looked scared and shaken.

Chapter 14
1995

The crowd

Only one stop.

Only one stop.

Finally, the artificial lighting of the approaching station took the place of the pseudo rural scenery.

"Fifty-ninth Street," the conductor announced. People, a crowd stepped on as I stepped off. Up and down the stairs, once again, to find an equally large group of people embarking upon the R, my train. I raced down the last few steps and ran full speed into the train just as the doors were closing. I was breathing heavily from the exertion but felt great relief to be among the crowd. Three stops later I was home.

Chapter 15
1995

The only daughter

Home, Eighty-sixth Street, Bay Ridge, Brooklyn. I walked down the main street, store fronts still lit despite their owners' absence. McDonalds was open as it always was, selling another twelve trillion crappy burgers to the unsuspecting public. The Korean deli on my corner was closed, but the identical one across the street was open. As I approached my apartment building, my eyes scanned the street for Roger's car. Sometimes he would be waiting for me when I came home. Tonight, he was nowhere to be found.

I entered my building. The lobby, instead of its usual scent of incense, smelled like dog, big wet dog, that distinct, rancid smell of a hound. The elevator seemed to take longer than usual. I belatedly remembered the mail as I awaited my floor. *The bills can sit until tomorrow*, I thought.

Leo scurried from the door as I walked into my apartment. He furiously sniffed my purse, laying on the small table as if trying to decipher where I had been all night. There were no messages, so where was Roger?

I hung up my jacket, took off my clothes, and looked around for something to get comfortable in.

I walked into the dressing room and covered my naked body with a long, midnight blue satin gown. To hell with the sweats, tonight I felt like satin. A peek into the fridge showed nothing very interesting except for the half jug of white wine left over from the past weekend. I poured myself a generous glass complete with ice cubes. Leo joined me in the kitchen in an affectionate mood. I scooped him up into my arms and adjusted the lighting to suit my state of mind. No TV, not tonight. I turned on the CD player and put on Rexx Camp, loud. The neighbors never complained.

Picking up my wine, I collapsed onto the couch, allowing the bewitching music to seep into my psyche. Leo joined me, taking his place on top of the cushion.

My gaze slowly transversed the room. Three pairs of eyes stared back. Green girl, regal girl and fed up, sick of life, leave-me-alone girl. Green girl was auburn haired, wavy luxurious long haired. She was dressed in a simple green velvet strapless dress, forever reaching her arm out for something. What she was reaching for I didn't know, she just wanted more. Only regal girl's head and neck showed. Her face was fixed in a knowing smile. Her aura was noble. She was satisfied. Fed up, sick of life, leave-me-alone girl warded off evil, pushing it vehemently back and away, as she took no nonsense, she was weary of nonsense and tired of being lied to. She was thick. I had used an excessive amount of paint on her, but she wore it well.

Their sisters and brothers resided in a stack in the foyer, and hung in the bathroom, and were rolled into tubes in the closet. Their newest sibling sat proudly against the far wall. She most closely resembled fed up, sick of life leave-me-alone girl. Her arms raised, fending off the dollar bills that rained down, upon her naked body. She was strong and could handle the brutalities of life.

"I'm getting cynical in my old age, Leo, nasty too. How about some candles, pussycat? We like candles, don't we? But we have to be careful not to burn our fur, okay?"

I took down a pair of candle sticks. Old wax had obscured some of the painted design on them, but I liked the way they looked, old and used and loved.

I took out two brand new tapered candles from the junk draw and set them up, just so.

Sitting back down on the couch I let the wine and the music work its magic as the day rolled out of my system, allowing the night to enter.

"Tonight is the first night of the rest of your life," I said to no one in particular and silently toasted Leo and the girls.

Thinking back on my day, I remembered the strange sort of daydream I had while on the train station. Mozart "Concerto #21." I got up, found the CD, and put it on endless repeat. I knew this music well, except I had no clue where it ended because I always put it on endless repeat. Making it a bit louder, I returned to the couch.

Head back, finally relaxed.

Roger, Dr. Kane, faces in front of my eyes, voices, and images. My hands began touching my body with a will of their own.

Fuck you, Roger. Who needs you?

A face, the man, the voice of my dreams.

Taking command.

Cassendre, my love.

The music, faster. Distant places, far off times. Flowing dresses and bodies waltzing. Faster, swirling, spinning.

Cassendre, my love.

131

HIS face grew larger in my mind's eye.

The music, gentle, floating down a slow river, the current pulling me along, the rapids up ahead.

Cassendre, my darling.

Whispered in my ear. Gentle arms holding me, my dark man guiding my movements. Feeling secure and loved.

Faster, stronger, the music coming to a crescendo and HIS presence faded away.

I turned off the CD. The small music box table next to the couch was pushed askew. Leo must have knocked into it, causing the photos on top to tumble out of place. My mom, looking happy and young, the shot taken at my cousin's wedding. I picked up the frame and brushed the dust from her smiling face. The next frame held a photo of my dad and I dancing at that same wedding. I missed him more and more each day. How satisfied he would have been to know that black holes really did exist. He had been a thinker, a book always in his hand. His life had been devoted to learning and understanding the sciences. My maternal grandmother and grandfather, both long gone. I had been everything to them, the youngest grandchild, their only daughter's only daughter. I missed them both terribly. Something inside the table was sticking out. I hadn't looked in there for ages. Taking all the frames off and placing them on the floor, I sat down and lifted the lid. Bittersweet, innocent notes emanated from the little table. Inside was a postcard from Italy from an old boyfriend, the Creation of Adam from the Sistine Chapel on front. That was what had been sticking out of the lid and had caught my eye. I reached in to see what else was inside.

A long strand of fake pearls, a single hoop earring and a photo folded in half, a Polaroid. I unfolded the picture and there was me and Beth Stone. How creepy. I looked so strange, my eyes red, my smile wicked. This shot was ten years old, almost to the day. The music box slowly wound down. I couldn't identify the tune. Reaching underneath the table, I turned the knob and the song started up again, strong and full. Each note lingered in the air, distinct from the one prior. Now I was able to tell what it was, "As Time is Here." I stared at the photo, remembering Lacy's the day it was taken.

Chapter 16
1985

The night ahead

"Cassidy, dinner's almost ready," my mother shouted from the kitchen.

I heard her but chose to ignore her, so intent I was on the sketch in front of me. A waist-length peplum gray flannel suit. Definitely with princess lines and a short slim skirt. Blind stitching on the hem, covered buttons. How the hell was I ever going to make this outfit by the end of the semester? Sketches of my term project were due after the holiday weekend. At FIT, we didn't have term papers, we had term projects.

"Cassidy, come eat, chop, chop, soup's on."

"Coming."

My father was already at the table, Aaron Simov in one hand, bread stick in the other.

"Harry, put the book down, I'm serving dinner."

"Okay, okay," He grumbled.

He placed the book next to his plate.

"Away, Harry, off the table."

"Alright, alright." He moved the book to the fourth empty seat under the place mat motioning shhhhhh with is finger and a wink to me. I giggled at my father's antics. Beer pot roast, one of my mother's specialties. Salad, potatoes. She sat down after placing the food on the table.

Dinner that night was somewhat subdued. The TV was on as usual, and the conversation centered on my mother's trip to the mall that afternoon and all the things she did not buy. None of us mentioned Uncle Neil.

The phone rang, and I raced from the table to answer it. It was Amber. We made plans to meet downstairs at the shopping center at eight o'clock.

"Where are you going tonight?" my mother asked as I resumed my place at the table.

"Out," I replied.

"Out, where?"

The phone rang again. I dropped my fork and ran to answer it, but no one was there.

"Wrong number," I said to my parents.

"I should have taken the phone off the hook, from now on that phone comes off the hook while we're eating dinner," my mother declared.

"So, Cassidy, out where?"

"Oh, I don't know, ma, just out with Amber, it *is* the night before Thanksgiving, you know, everybody's going out."

I glanced up at the clock opposite the kitchen table.

"Out to that bar? You're not old enough to even walk in that place—"

"But we hang out outside, ma, it's still warm enough, and I will be eighteen this week."

"Sylvia—" My dad interjected, coming to my rescue.

"She's a responsible girl, let her go out with her friends."

"Thank you, dad."

I looked up at the clock again.

"Look at her, she can't wait to go running. Finish your dinner first, Cassidy."

"I am, I'm finished, I'm going to get ready."

I cleaned my plate and went to get showered and ready for the night ahead.

Chapter 17
1985

The emergence of
the pool player

Eight o'clock, the shopping center. Old man Spiegel limping down the stretch muttering to himself. The E Shack getting prepared to close shop for the night. Mr. Gold carrying home bagels for his invalid wife. Neighborhood people doing their neighborhood thing. I stood at the bank waiting for Amber.

Honkkkkkk—

Amber pulled up in her brother's van. The vehicle was big enough to fit eight people and looked much too large for such a tiny girl like Amber to drive. She handled it as if it were a Trans Am.

"Cass— C'mon, get in, let's go! Don't lock the door!"

The Stein family never locked the doors of the van. The locks had broken some time ago and her brother had never gotten around to fixing them. Besides, no one would want to steal the van. It looked very unappealing and had nothing very interesting in it.

"I know, I know, I won't lock the door."

"What's up, Cassidy, how do I look? You like my eye makeup?"

She turned to me, closing her eyes for a moment.

"Amb— C'mon, you're driving for Christ's sake, you want to get us killed?"

"Don't worry, I've got it under control."

She cut over to the left-hand lane and pulled up to a red light at Ocean Parkway.

"Let me see," I said. "Now you can close your eyes, we're not moving."

She smiled, turned to me, eyes closed, lips puckered.

"Well, what do you think?"

"I love it, finally you listened to me and bought a black eyeliner. I can't believe it. You think Johnny will be there?"

"I don't know," she said with a broad grin and a singsong voice.

Her ocean blue eyes lit up at the mention of Johnny. She brushed back her long dark hair and popped a piece of gum into her mouth.

"Want?"

"No, thanks. By the way, the light's not going to get any greener."

She put the van into motion, driving up Neptune Avenue.

"My mom wants to know if you're coming for Thanksgiving dinner tomorrow?" I said.

"Who's going to be there?"

"Just us and my Uncle Neil."

"Yeah, I'll be there, tell your mom to make me some pineapple chicken, okay?"

"Yeah, right—you tell her—did you bring the pot?"

"Got it, right here." She pointed to her small purse laying next to her on the driver's seat.

"Did you bring the papers?" she asked me.

"Got it, right here." I said pointing to my own small purse in my lap.

"Let's hear some tunes," I said, suddenly yearning to hear the radio.

She reached forward to turn it on. The reception wasn't very clear and kept fading in and out as we drove down the broken streets of Brooklyn. Our destination was Captain Wakers, a large bar on the dock in Sheepshead Bay. Usually we would get to The Bay early; it was only a ten-minute drive from the neighborhood. By nine o'clock or so a crowd would be forming outside the bar, friends, high school buddies— everyone just hanging out. Sometimes we went into the bar, only when a certain bouncer, Artie, was on duty. He didn't care that we weren't old enough to be drinking inside. Our phony ID was good enough for him. If Artie was there we'd smile, flash our doctored birth certificates, and make a night of it in Captain Wakers.

"Cass, can you fix this damn thing?" She was fiddling with the tuner. I reached for the knob, trying to find some clear music. Up and down the dial. Watching the red line indicator move back and forth, back and forth.

Anything, any music would do, I needed to hear music, NOW! Static, voices...

"Cassidy! Hello! Wake up, what's the matter with you? You zoning on me? We haven't even smoked yet--"

She snapped her fingers in front of my face.

"I'm okay, I said, shutting the radio off.

"Hey, Cass— what's the matter?"

"Nothing, never mind."

"Tell me—"

"No, really, nothing."

"What did you do today?"

For a moment I couldn't remember. Then it all came back, the trip to Lacy's, the BMA Building..."

"Not much," I replied.

143

She pulled into a spot on Emmons Avenue.
"You sure you're okay?"
"Yeah— I'm sure."
I took out the rolling paper and gave her a sheet, she folded it three quarters of the way before the gummed edge.
Thoughts

She took out three pinches of weed from the small plastic bag.

Thoughts were coming rapidly

She slowly folded over the edge of the paper and pressed the pot into the fold.

Thoughts were coming rapidly, too many to focus
So Many
Bouncing off the walls of my brain
My mind
DO NOT LOCK THE DOORS
By any reasonable logic that ticks in your mind
Beware of the incense, it's not always kind

She rolled, fingers spread, up the length of the paper, back-tracking and rolling up again.

Oh Please look on through
But by God— Do not jump
Don't Holler or whimper
Or yell or stand up

She licked the gummed strip

I am
I am listening
And judging and weighing
So here I stand
Hoping, rejoicing, and praying

Pressing the wet paper into the tuft of weed.

To take back my lover
Back into my arms
To worship, to cherish
And taste of her charms

"Cass— Cassidy, look, it's perfect."
She knocked into me with her elbow.
"What?"
"Cassidy, wake up, look at this joint I just rolled, it's perfect."
She held the joint out for my inspection.
"Light it, I want to smoke."
"Not in my brother's van, what are you crazy? You know I can't smoke in here, he'll kill me—"
I already had the match lit. I held it to the end of the joint and inhaled slowly, taking the smoke deep onto my lungs and closing my eyes. The match died out in my hand.
"You're such an asshole sometimes. Roll down your window, will you? Give it to me!"
She grabbed it from my hand took a hit and put it out and back into her purse.

"Let's go."

We parked the van. We shut the windows but did not lock the doors.

Crossing the street heading towards Wakers Dock, we could already see friends waving to us from the benches outside the bar. Elise, Lisa, Alice, Susan, Tracey and Dana were laughing, standing outside the doors.

"Hey you!" Elise called. "You guys going in? We'll be in soon."

The night was chilly, colder than I had expected. Artie the bouncer stood watch in front, allowing us to enter. A four-piece band played loudly in the back while the crowd of young people with beer bottles in hand shouted to each other over the rock music. Amber spotted Johnny sitting on a stool opposite the front door and made a beeline for him, leaving me standing alone.

I walked over to the pool table where a game was winding down. A group of bikers stood around the table. One of them, a muscular, shaven haired guy with tattoos up and down his arms waited his turn while his friend, who was equally muscular and tattooed, proceeded to clear the table. The diamond stud in his ear picked up the light from above the table and glittered as he slammed the remaining eight ball into the corner pocket.

"Yeah!—" he shouted, taking a swig of beer from his bottle of Bud.

"Alright, Joe, drinks on you for the rest of the night, cheers." He tilted his head back and downed the last of his beer.

"I'll have me a shot of tequila and another Bud, buddy." He laughed, flinging the empty bottle into a beer bottle filled garbage can against the wall.

Joe took out his wallet and headed off to the crowded bar without a word.

"Hey pretty lady, c'mon and play a game with me, Joe ain't gonna be back for a while."

He was racking up the balls, setting the table for a new game. He walked over to me, cue stick in his hand and put his arm around my shoulders.

"What's your name, pretty lady?"

"Cassidy."

"Cassidy, I'm Dean, damn nice to meet you." He let go of my shoulders and held out his hand. We shook.

"Cassidy, what are you drinking tonight?"

"I'll have a Bud."

"Ah, a girl after my own heart." He turned to one of his friends.

"Hey, you— go tell Joe to get my friend Cassidy here a Bud."

His friend disappeared into the crowd in search of Joe.

"You ever play pool before?" he asked me.

"Once or twice."

"You know the rules, don't you? It's simple. I break. Whoever gets in a ball first, that's what color balls they are, stripes or solids. You gotta get in all your balls and then call the eight—you got it?"

"I got it."

He held out the cue stick for me to take.

"Here's your stick, here's your chalk— let's play."

He walked to the head of the table, bending low to visually line up the cue ball. He stepped back and swung the stick hard against the ball. The stack of balls exploded going in all directions, but none went in.

"Nice break, Dean, why don't you get a few balls in next time?" his other friend said, lighting a cigarette.

Dean walked over and took the cigarette out of his hand taking a drag.

"Yeah, asshole, next time it'll be your head instead of that cue ball—pretty lady, it's your turn."

He stepped in back of me, putting his arms around to show me how to hold the stick.

"Just hold the front real tight and secure with your fingers like this and slide the stick back and forth till it feels just right—then POW! Slam it."

He smashed his fist into his palm.

I bent over, concentrating on hitting the white ball. Pulling back the stick and aiming for a number nine, a stripe, I hit it sending the cue spinning forward but hitting nothing.

"That's OK, nice try, I go—"

He chalked up and walked around to the other side of the table. Bending low, examining the set-up from all angles, he raised the stick and slammed it into the cue. The balls scattered into each other but again none went in.

"Doing great there, Dean—" His friend started to say but was silenced by Dean's withering look.

"Don't even try it, fool," Dean said to him. Joe had returned with the drinks. Dean took the two Buds and the shot of tequila from Joe's hand and handed me my beer.

"Chin-Don, a thousand years." He toasted me and swallowed the tequila in one move, chasing it with the beer, and I drank in response to his cheer.

"Your turn," Dean said.

I stepped up to the table, staring at the cue.

I felt
HIS presence
I bent down and hit a perfect shot. Knowing it was right, feeling it, willing the ball to go directly into the corner pocket.
I'm here
I am with you
My lady
My love
I moved into position to hit the next solid ball.
Be strong
And shine proud
Like the stars up above
Bang! The ball shot into the side pocket.
I'm leading
I'm guiding
The stones are in place
Bang! Another one—off the bank and into the pocket.
To surround you
with diamonds
with pearls
And with lace
Again! Smooth. A perfect shot.
"You sure you ain't never played this game before, pretty lady? You're either damn good or damn lucky."
"She's whippin' your butt, Dean."
The guys were all standing around, watching my game.
"I'm just feeling very lucky tonight," I said.
I chalked my cue stick and stepped back to see what was left for me to hit. Three more balls. Bang! Two more. Slow, perfect. One more, the eight ball.

His striped balls remained, untouched on the green felt. I chalked up again. The game had been effortless. HE was with me. I leaned over, intent on hitting the final shot. Slowly. Carefully, I missed. The white cue fell a quarter of an inch shy of its target.

"I thought I was done for sure." Dean came over to stand next to me, chalking up.

"My turn." He bent over, pumped twice with the stick and slammed into the cue with a vengeance. The balls scattered across the table but when they came to rest not one had gone into a pocket.

"What the fuck is going on here?"

"Dean, man you got a lot of balls, on the table I mean."

"Shut up asshole, I taught this little lady everything she knows about playin' pool, right?" His hand traced a circle on my shoulder. I pulled away, chalk in hand, rubbing it across the head of the stick. I looked up at him, smiling sweetly.

"Yes, but now it's my turn."

He had left the balls randomly spread about. The black eight ball resided near the far corner pocket.

I circled the table, chalk still in hand. The only shot possible was a straight line diagonally. It would be a tight squeeze and had to be done perfectly or not at all.

"I have to call it, right Dean?"

"You're gonna make her call it?" a peanut said from the gallery.

"Rules are rules." He stared into my eyes as he took a swig of beer.

"Eight ball in the corner pocket!"

I bent down.

Cue ball dead center.

My princess of darkness
My midnight Rapunzel
come feed on my yearning
extinguish this candle

Slowly, I hit the ball. One shot. Boom, across the table, into the eight ball and on into the hole. Ahhhhh, perfection.

I stood up victoriously and went to shake Dean's hand.

"Dean, what can I say? It's been an experience."

"Anytime, pretty lady, anytime."

"Hey—" He called to me as I was walking away. "You want the table? It's yours, you won, and rules are rules."

are rules

are rules

Amber, where was that little shit? Probably off making out with John-ny in some dark corner. Out of my way—Excuse me, Jeez can they let some more people in here? Excuse me! Blondie, can you move your fat ass, can't you see me coming through? Didn't you watch me put that baboon to shame? I. I am the leading lady, I AM Marilyn Monroe. This is MY night and MY gig. He's cute. Is he smiling at me? —He's not cute enough. I can get better. Look at her—I'm prettier than her—OH GOD—look at her outfit—I'll give her the evil eye for daring to wear such a horrific assemblage of garments to my —

to my

to my

gathering!

MY PARTY—MINE—MINE—MINE—Where is HE, I smell HIM—I know HE's here, and what has HE done this time? What mischief has HE stepped his tail into now...to expect me to withdraw HIM from when

HE bellows my name CESSENDRE! —

Wench – woman, I need to use the royal facilities, would it be too much of a bother to step aside and let a lady pass, a real lady, not that the lowly likes of you would recognize a woman of worth if she punched you in the ribs—Move—MOve—MOVE—

Oh please, won't you move, all of you I have to pee, I shall wet my pants.

Such earthy nonsense— This constant flow of LIFE— into the mouth and out of the rump. Endless, tiresome, to be executed every few hours, no less. I'll just kick this door shut and take my sweet time.

Ahhhhhhhhh, time.

Coming!— Damn HIM. Why must HE always call for me in my most intimate of moments.

Hmmmmmmm, there now, that feels good.

Ahhhhhhhhhhhhhhhhhhh—That feels even better. What flight of fancy shall it be this time? What track shall I set my mind loose upon? But the question of the evening is which finger will be the lucky chosen one to frolic when the juices come?

Ahhhhhhhhhhhh, the place, I've found it. Precisely where I knew it would be.

Alright, ALLRIGHT—

Darling, join me, in here, it IS so very lovely, and the night is still so young. Yes, oh, yes, my handsome demon. Do come when I call. Dearest one. Shall we be dancing tonight or walking the hounds? Will we be flying? Can you fetch my cloak? Or should I run to get my Black leather, Baby? C'mon, tell mama what the problem is. Where are you? Come out, come out, wherever you are.

Never mind, – forgive me but humanity gives me arrogance.

My fingers will suffice— for now.

Stay where you are,

YOU ARE NOT WANTED.

Chapter 18
1985

Giving Thanks

Thanksgiving

"Cassidy, where are you? Our guests will be here soon."

I heard my mother from my bedroom but didn't answer. I continued putting on my eye makeup, standing in front of the full-length mirror on the back of my door. Eyeliner, two coats of mascara, separating it with my trusty safety pin, a dash of blush, lipstick, of course, to please Mom and I was done. I adjusted my black sweater and flung my head upside down three times to fluff my hair and I was finished.

"Coming Mom," I yelled.

I walked into the dining room.

"You look lovely, pussycat," my father said.

I smiled at him.

"Thanks, Dad."

"Cassidy, get the cranberry sauce and the glasses and put them on the table."

"Yes, Mom."

The doorbell rang.

I opened the door and there stood Uncle Neil.

"Hey there, beautiful, come here and hug your Uncle Neil."

He took me into his arms and gave me a gigantic hug.

I wormed my way out of his embrace and closed the door behind him. Taking the bottle of wine from his hand, I put it on the table and took his coat into my bedroom.

"Come in, Neil," my mom called from the kitchen.

He sat down on the couch, making himself comfortable.

"So, how is everything?" he said, pointing his nose to my father.

They busied themselves with small talk as my mother and I finished setting the table. I retrieved two bottles of wine from the cabinet plus the bottle that Uncle Neil had brought.

The doorbell rang.

I ran to open the door to find Amber standing there with a large bouquet of flowers.

"Thank God you're here," I said.

She blinked her ocean blue eyes and said, "I'm here." with a laugh.

I put her jacket on my bed and returned to the party.

"Hello beautiful," Uncle Neil said with a big hug to Amber. Amber sat down on the couch and joined in the small talk.

The weather.

The politics.

Uncle Neil's return from Colorado.

Finally, my mother declared, "Dinner is ready."

We all found our places in the dining room.

The flowers that Amber had brought took the center. My mother proudly put the cut-up turkey on the table.

"Let's eat," she said.

We passed the turkey, potatoes, cranberry sauce, string bean casserole, bread, stuffing.

Finally, our glasses were filled with wine. The small talk continued.

"Neil, are you happy to be home?" my mother asked.

"Home is where the heart is. Yes, I'm happy to be home near my family."

"Did you like Colorado?" Amber asked.

"Well, the scenery was beautiful, breathtaking really, the folks were friendly, but nothing is like New York, especially Brooklyn. Seven years was a long time."

We ate and drank and I ate and drank and drank because no one was paying attention to me. I was sitting next to Uncle Neil. He and I shared another open bottle of wine.

I leaned over to Uncle Neil and whispered–

"You were on the TV – yes?"

I cut into my turkey, looking around the table to see who was listening.

"You were on the TV– yes?"

I cut deeper into my turkey.

"You were on the telethon, yes?" I whispered.

He looked at me, fork in his hand.

"What? What are you talking about, my beautiful niece?"

We continued eating and drinking.

"I saw you," I whispered to him, digging into the stuffing.

He looked at me as if I were crazy.

"Amber, I saw him," I said loudly.

She looked at me with wide eyes.

"I SAW YOU." I screamed.

Everyone stopped in their tracks.

Where ever you go

Every seed you sow

Know that I'm with you

"I SAW YOU."

I dropped my fork and knife and ran into my room and slammed the door so hard that the mirror on my door cracked and splintered into a multitude of pieces. I held the door shut, hearing my mother approaching.

My mother tried to open the door.

"Cassidy, open this door immediately."

"No," I said.

"Cassidy, I said OPEN THIS DOOR."

"No," I said.

"This is your last chance. NOW OPEN THIS DOOR."

I opened the door to let her in. She took a look around at the pieces of the mirror strewn about the rug.

"That's it," she said. "We're going to the doctor."

Chapter 19
1995

I pray the Lord

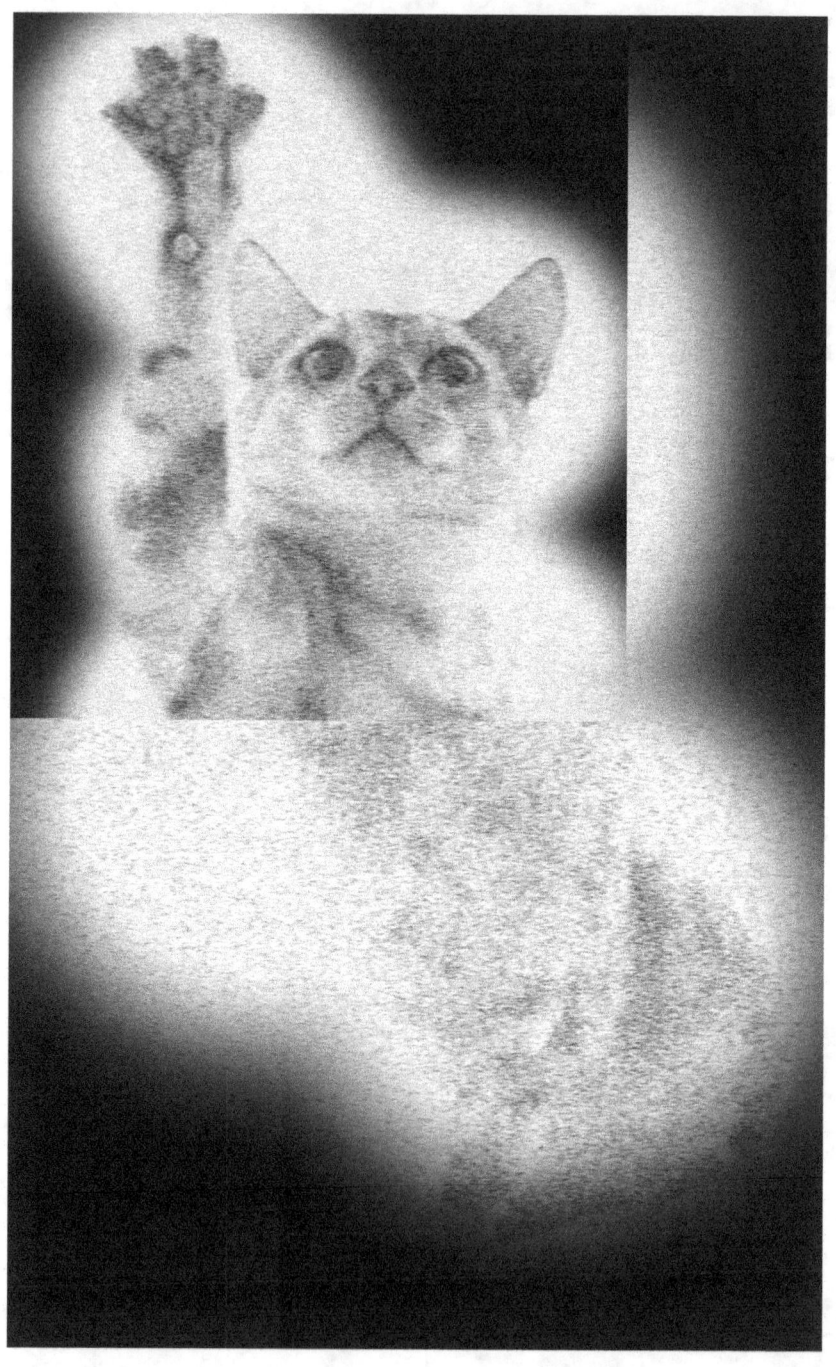

Owwwwwwwwww—

"Leo, what? What do you want pussycat?

What are you biting Mama for?"

I put the polaroid back into the music box.

"C'mon darling, let's get to bed. Enough is enough for one night."

I picked up my animal and placed him back in his spot on the couch. The couch would do for tonight. I took blankets and pillows from the closet and made a comfortable nest for myself. Lights out. Goodnight Roger, wherever you are. Sleep tight.

Now I lay me down to sleep.

I pray the lord my soul to keep.

Damn, my pills. The kitchen seemed so far away.One night of missed pills wouldn't kill me.

I pray the lord my soul to keep.

If I should die before I wake.

I pray the lord my soul to take.

Chapter 20
1995

Timing Logic Rhythm

Saturday

What?

I awoke from a dead sleep. Dead, no dreams.

Ahhhhhhh. Stretching, yawning, turning, pulling off the sweet nighttime threads that had entwined my body. My back hurt. That certain pang that came from spending the night on the pull-out couch. Gingerly, I got up heading straight for the bathroom. Leo joined me and came to sit on my lap as I passed the delicious first pee of the morning.

"What's up pussycat," I sang to him.

"Mama's going to the city today." I had just decided. "Mama's not going to sit home and wait for Roger to call, she's going to have a lovely day all by herself."

I deposited Leo on to the floor and stomped off into the kitchen.

"Come, pussycat, breakfast."

I dipped my hand into Leo's container of food and dumped a handful into his bowl. He jumped up onto the counter and began to munch loudly. I picked up the phone to call my mother.

The clock started to chime as I dialed. I loved that clock; Roger hated it. It looked like an old school clock encased in mahogany wood. The pendulum gained a few minutes each month and needed to be adjusted. I had bought it at a Salvation Army store for twenty three dollars. It chimed once on the half hour and once for each hour on the hour.

I dialed my mother. I put down the receiver to listen to the clock, taking pleasure in listening to the tones. Once, twice, three times, again and again. Ten o'clock.

I dialed my mother again. She answered on the first ring.

"Hello."

"Hi, ma."

"Did you just call?"

I hesitated.

"No." Why was I lying to my mother? I was certainly an evil child.

"What are you doing today?" she asked me. "I have nothing to do. Do you want to meet me?"

"No, ma, I have something to take care of."

"What?"

"I have to go to the library and research something for work."

Lies, lies. I was lying to my mother for no good reason.

"Really?"

"Yes, really. I'll call you later, okay?"

"Okay, Cassidy, go ahead, do what you have to do. I'll just stay home and play with myself."

"What? What did you say?"

"I said I'll just stay home and keep myself busy while you go off and have a good time."

"Always, do you always have to make me feel guilty?"

"That's only your insecurities talking, Cassidy, it's not me."

"Okay, I'll speak to you later. Bye."

"Goodbye."

I slammed down the receiver, stifling my guilt.

"Today is my day!" I declared, suddenly feeling light, young and carefree.

I quickly showered, got dressed and ready to leave.

Walking down Eighty-sixth Street, I was planning my day. The shopping crowd was gathered early, for it was just about noon. The Thanksgiving holiday this week would be bringing them out in droves. The drug store was unusually warm and stuffy when I walked in and went directly to the stationary section.

I needed a new notebook.

I picked up a two-subject book. No, I didn't like the divider. Maybe a five subject? No, I don't want subjects. Here was a thick, three hundred pager. Looking at it closely I decided I didn't want lines. I wanted a non-lined notebook, but I couldn't find one, and I didn't want a drawing pad. On second thought, maybe the two-subject book would do. This is ridiculous. I took it to the register and paid for it. I had a pen with me; I always did.

The subway station was deserted. Obviously I had just missed a train. I held tightly onto my new notebook, wanting to wait until I was seated and settled for the ride until I cracked it open. My destination was West Eighth Street. I was in the mood for The Village. Finally some people joined me at the station and the train came. I settled into my corner seat in the middle of the train where the conductor stood.

A new notebook. How I loved a new notebook. I opened it up and stared at the pristine white pages with delicate light blue lines. Pen in hand, I wondered what to put on the page. Should I write, just write my thoughts, or should I dig deep and create a poem? Should I draw? Maybe doodle?

I closed my eyes, getting into the motion of the train. Looking out at the blackness of the tunnel, seeing labyrinths and passageways, a face. I let my pen rest on the page.

Ovals

Eyes

A face.

The face was appearing on my page.

Dark near the eyes. Angled by the neck. A slant to the eyebrows. The nose sharp and dignified and oh— a strong jaw with a slight shadow hugging the contours. No, not only a shadow, a small goatee with a hint of a cleft. Lips pursed in an almost smile. The neck, tilted more, causing the shoulders to be slightly uneven. HIS hairline began with a widow's peak, long, straight locks came to rest upon those uneven shoulders. The hollow in HIS checks needed more definition, as did HIS eyes.

The man looking out from my page was the man from my dreams. And how beautiful HE was; regal, imposing, demanding. HEstared defiantly back at me, trapped within the confines of the paper.

I gazed back out the window.

"West Eighth Street next stop," the conductor announced.

I ascended from the hot train station to find that clouds had taken over the sky. Just the kind of day I liked, somewhat overcast, a tease of rain in the air without being a real threat. Undecided as to exactly which direction to take, I started walking south on Broadway, towards Soho.

Without much money in my pocket I couldn't do any serious shopping, so I needed to find an ATM machine somewhere along my way. Window shopping would have to do for now, lusting after all the beautiful things I could not buy. Money really did make the world go 'round. If the craziest man had a fortune at home he would be eccentric, not crazy. If Roger had an amazing job we could be a normal couple and get married, not this fighting bullshit which was basically generated by our lack of money. So where was Roger? Last I had seen or heard from him was Thursday night, today was Saturday. I just couldn't understand him. Where did he disappear to? He pulled this on me all the time. I would see him for a stretch, maybe a week and then "poof" he'd vanish for days. Where did he go? When he did finally come back a fight was inevitable. He would artfully dodge my questions with flippant answers or skillfully change the subject, leaving me aggravated and frustrated. Frustrated like I was now, because I had no money to spend. Why did I stay with this annoying creature?

Enough, I was not going to ruin my day by ruminating on Roger's antics. Whatever will be will be, que sera, sera, Cassidy.

This block was boring me. I turned off Broadway and made my way to Bleeker Street and took a table in a cafe to treat myself to lunch. I took out my new notebook while waiting for my meal to arrive. Turning to a new page, I saw a vision in my mind and quickly sketched in the outline so as not to lose the exact position of the figure I imagined.

HE sat reclined, in his chair, HIS legs spread slightly, HIS right hand resting under his chin, HIS long hair falling forward and coming to rest upon his chest. HIS left hand was reaching out to accept something. Strong broad strokes. The chair supporting HIM was taking shape and form. Shadows, contours. HIS face was tilted, his body at a relaxed angle. The basic sketch was there, and I began drawing in the details. HE was wearing a robe, a green velvet robe that hung slightly open and draped over one knee. Underneath HE had on pants only, HIS strong chest muscles were slightly visible. The sleeves came to halfway down HIS arm and...

"Excuse me, but that's a beautiful drawing you're making."

I turned to see an elderly woman. She looked to be in her mid-eighties. Her hair was silver gray and tucked up elegantly into her smart black hat. She sat alone at the table next to me, a cup of coffee in front of her. Her well-tailored red suit had Chanel buttons down the front and one good look at her told me those were real. White kid gloves rested primly in her lap next to her black patent leather purse. She seemed to have stepped out of another time and place.

"I used to be somewhat of an artist myself, but that was years ago."

"Really? What kind of an artist?"

"Oh, a little of this and a little of that. I dabbled in sculpture for a while, but my passion was painting."

"Oils? Acrylics?"

"Both, depending upon my mood, of course. I loved the immediacy of the acrylics, the instant gratification —ahhhhhh, but the sensuality of the oils, now that is where a true painter's heart lies."

Those were my feelings, exactly.

"I know what you mean," I said.

"Of course you do, my dear. Why don't you come over to my table and take your lunch with me?"

I moved over to her table just as the waiter was serving my food.

"What perfect timing, life is all about timing, you know, you should remember that."

I sat down.

"Go ahead, eat, don't be shy on my account."

I picked up my fork and began eating my lunch as I was very hungry.

"You eat, I'll talk. Now where was I, oh, yes, timing. I do believe there are certain things in life that are just more important than others, don't you agree?"

"Yes, of course," I said, looking for something to wipe my mouth with.

"For some it may be their families or their jobs, here, take my napkin—"

"Thank you."

"But things like families and jobs are of obvious importance to everyone."

She took a delicate sip of her coffee. "Yes?"

"I never really thought about it."

We shared a comfortable silence for a few moments. She looked a little sad and lost sitting there in her Sunday best watching the locals walk by. Maybe that was just my warped perception of her, or my own insecurities as my mother would put it.

"What I meant to say was that to me, the important things, the ones that matter up here." She tapped her forehead with a wrinkled finger.

"And in here." She tapped on her chest.

"Are three." She held out her hand with her first three fingers out like a child telling her age.

"I've given this subject much thought you know."

"Three?"

"Yes, three. The three most important things in life are timing, rhythm, and logic. And of those three the most important of them all is timing."

She stopped to signal the waiter for a refill of her coffee, and I picked at my food, waiting for her to continue.

"You either have timing or you don't." She stirred her black coffee.

"It's the closest of the three to luck and that you're either born with or you're not. You know what I mean? Now rhythm and logic are a little harder to explain. Rhythm, hmmmmm, rhythm is about a person's highs and lows, let's see, you must know how a woman has a pretty spell followed by an ugly week or two, it comes and goes, ebbs and flows. Or how 'bout when you're on a roll and things are going right and everything is falling into place and how good it feels? It's rhythm. It's your highs and lows and when the highs are high they're right there in your face and when the lows come in you're scared silly that Mr. High is just not coming back. And oh! How you try to coax Mr. High back into your kitchen but he just takes his own sweet time, selfish demon that he is. And I know you understand what I'm telling you, young lady. I don't even know your name and you don't know mine, and I'm not sitting here but five minutes talking to you, but I see in your eyes that you know what I'm talking about."

I put down the last of my lunch, suddenly not very hungry anymore.

"It's the creative demon, it is." She pointed a finger at me in a scolding tone.

"He's a hungry puppy. But that is where logic comes in because without logic, timing and rhythm are lost. Without someone to guide timing and rhythm they become grains of sand lost with the others on the beach. Logic is beauty and it is the soft yarn that binds our souls together. Understand?"

She picked up her cup and signaled with it to the waiter for her check.

I understood.

"I know you do. You've still got some way to go, young lady, but you'll be fine, I see it in your eyes."

She stood up, gathering her gloves and purse into her hand and reaching behind her for a cane that I hadn't seen before.

"You have yourself a sweet life." She smiled and turned and walked out of the cafe.

Timing.
Logic.
Rhythm.
I paid my bill and left the restaurant.

Walking.
Timing
Logic.
Rhythm.

Windows, damn, I wanted to shop.

Women in windows, standing and posing for me. Mocking me with their promises of beautiful possessions.

Logic.

I haven't any money, so therefore I cannot shop.

Walking, moving to the beat of the crowded city streets. Dogs, and people and posters and thieves. Riches surrounding me, but yet I cannot steal.

Rhythm.

Timing.

So, dearest one, is timing luck or is luck timing? Has our time come? I search for you, I hear you calling for me, but yet I fear it is not right. The dogs, have they been fed? Has the beast awoken? Is he ready to feast? Or is he reluctant to bend? These God forsaken vehicles that surround me now, ahhhhhhhh! Let them make their blessed way to their destinations and leave me be. So many people, why do I always find myself in the midst of a crowd? How I long for our dark countryside, somewhere for me to extend my arms wide and find nothing and no one there, to run full force when I take off for flight and not collide with these, these...people. Dear God, they are everywhere. They sleep in the streets, they gather in taverns, they seem to have a need for close contact at all times. For the life of me I cannot understand where they all came from. And Oh! They are so ugly! Yes, I know, I must be kind and remember this is the end of the twentieth century and I know, I must behave and act like the good girl that we both know I'm not. Dearest one, is this last page of the millennium treating you kindly? It can be quite fun once my heart stops pounding from fear of these creatures. Have I mentioned they smell, too? I suppose I rather do enjoy the sight of these monster structures, these office buildings. So smooth they look and when the sun bounces off them at a certain angle—mama-mia— our own Vincent could not throw such sharp daggers. And what of these flying mechanical birds that I see crossing the skies and trailing such noise. They hold people in their bellies, bunches of them sitting comfortably in their innards.

I have been asleep it seems for so long. I have found these modern wonders, these talking boxes controlled by magic wands. But I have not forgotten you, my love, your strong arms nor your words of wisdom. And I shall heed to the rules of this game that we play. So, in keeping with the rules I sadly declare—no, my treasure. Although I hear you calling for me, our time has not come, not yet.

The hour is still mine, MINE, MINE, MINE. I stamp my feet and shout to the sky and yes, I carry on as a child. It is my prerogative as a woman to do so.

Oh dearest one, I am feeling positively wicked this afternoon. These women in windows, they go, they do, they taunt me and mock me and say such evil things to me, speaking to me with only their eyes. They are, they're jealous that I am free to roam and wander and dance if I must, while they are trapped behind those great panes of glass.

Cassendre
they whisper
so softly that no mortals hear
We're watching
they stare at me
slyly so no mortals see

So, WAIT, I reply, it is not within my power to help you, rotten wenches that you once were and will always be. Filthy whores, the whole lot of you. Suffer, you obviously deserve to.

Did you not know the rules? You poor creatures—had you no vision at all? Pity on you for your lack of foresight and more importantly for your absence of faith.

I am growing weary, lover. My energy is not up to par as of yet. But there seems to be nowhere to escape to. Out of my way, peasant, I see a cave.

Darling, I feel you near. Your energy is warming me, and I am comforted by the presence of your all-encompassing love.

Ahhhhh, the cave is almost within reach and just in time...
in logic...
in rhythm...

Chapter 21
1995

Prince Charming

I slowly walked down the steps of the subway station as an "R" train pulled up to the platform. I took my seat and rested my head on the filthy glass, tired and longing to be home. A heaviness filled my heart as I gazed at the yellow handrail lining the wall of the underground tunnel. The lights passing above my head in the darkness looked like a flashing warning signal. Blinking on and off, on and off. A warning was too late at this point, because I knew already that something was wrong and the horror was here. I closed my eyes in an effort to turn off my brain and fell into a solid sleep.

Eighty-sixth Street. I awoke and made my way upstairs to the street, softened by the aura of the fog. I just wanted to get home. Stopping by the pet shop window. Puppies dancing and prancing and being brutal to one another.

I went upstairs, throwing my new notebook aside. Sleep. I just wanted to sleep. Leo came to accompany me on my journey to never-never land. No message from Roger on the machine. I closed my eyes and rested.

The downstairs bell woke me at eight fourteen. I know it was eight fourteen because the first place I looked when it rang was the clock.

Groggily, I made my way to the buzzer.

"Who is it?"

"Hello love, it's Prince Charming, don't be afraid."

I buzzed Roger in.

Prince charming, my ass, I thought as I waited for him to arrive. I heard the elevator open and heavy footsteps coming down the hall. I opened the door before he had a chance to ring.

"Cassidy, baby, I love you, I missed you."

He grabbed me into his arms.

"Give me a kiss—"

I struggled out of his embrace.

"Roger, stop."

"C'mon— Cass, don't be mad at me, I've got presents for you!"

"I'm not interested."

"Fine, you want to be—"

"Roger, look, let me put it this way. I am so fed up with you and your nonsense. I've told you this over and over. If you want to be with me you've got to grow up--g-r-o-w-u-p--can I spell it out for you any clearer? I don't have the time nor the will to deal with your bullshit!"

"Go ahead."

"Go ahead? I will— my time is just too precious to me to waste on wondering where you are, or what you are doing or what trouble you're in at the moment or what time you're coming back, or, or—"

He walked into the kitchen and opened a beer.

"Keep going Cass, if it makes you feel any better, then vent all you want."

I think the smug look on his face is what really sent me over the edge.

"Listen you son of a bitch, I have had it with you— you think this is a joke, it's not— If you refuse to grow up and take responsibility for your actions, then I'm just not going to have anything to do with you, do you understand? BY GOD, do you understand what I'm saying? I can't stand you anymore, the way you breathe makes me sick— you repulse me with your ignorance and your behavior is nauseating."

I was trembling with indignation.

"Calm down," he said.

"You and I are through."

"CALM DOWN," he screamed, rage in his voice and upon his face.

I stormed off into the bathroom because there was no other room to run to. I heard him put the television on inside, which made me even more angry. I pulled open the door and went back to face him. Clapping twice to shut the TV with that stupid clapper I stood there breathing hard.

Flash

"Roger—"

Flash

Red

That face—

"Roger!"

Thoughts were coming rapidly, too many to focus.

"Rogerrrrrrr!"

He stood up, reaching for me, his persona changing to concern.

"What's the matter, Cassidy, honey!"

He was holding me, trying to comfort me.

"Rog, it's happening, it's happening again, oh my god!" I pulled free from his arms.

"Roger, I'm scared. I think I'm getting sick again. I can't take it, not again. What should I do? Please help me, this can't happen again. I can't take it."

He gathered me into his arms once more and held me and stroked my head while I cried.

"Cass, listen, you've got to go see Dr. Bloom."

"I did, I mean I called him the other day, that was yesterday, it feels like weeks ago."

"What happened? Why didn't you tell me?"

"I, I don't know where to begin. The other day, Thursday, I was coming home in my cab and I, I just felt funny, the radio was funny, you know? And then on the way home from the city, I was scared, no, oh, yeah, then my screen saver, no, I don't know, I called Dr. Bloom but he wasn't there, he's away, he's on vacation and there was another doctor there, Dr. Kane, Vincent Kane, and he took my blood, and he told me to wait till the results came back on Wednesday."

"What else did he say?"

"He said that he just thought I was working too hard and that I was too stressed out and that he didn't think I was getting sick again, and I didn't take my medicine last night—"

"Why didn't you take it?"

"I don't know, I was in bed and I was so comfortable, and I didn't want to get up—

"Are you crazy?"

"Don't scream at me, I'm sorry. I'm scared."

"Ah, baby, don't be scared. I'm the one who is sorry. I should have been here for you." He stroked my back.

"Listen—" He held my head between his hands.

"You are going to be fine. Just think, you've been working your butt off lately, not to mention putting up with my bullshit which would make anyone koo koo— you just need to take it easy." Ding dong, the clocked chimed eight-thirty.

"Ahhhhhh," I screamed at the noise and we both started to laugh.

"Oh baby, I promise I'm going to be so good to you from now on. You just need me to take better care of you, you will be fine, do you hear me?"

I nodded yes, gazing up at him.

"You have to go back Wednesday?"

"Yes."

"Well, I'm going with you. I'm sure he'll tell you that it's nothing and that you have to start eating right and going to bed at a decent hour and taking it easy at work and taking better care of yourself. Shit, he'll probably tell you that you have to get rid of me."

"Never, Roger, I could never get rid of you.

He traced the path of my tears first with his finger and then with his tongue. Slowly he lowered me down onto my knees. Kissing my neck, opening my shirt and kissing me on my shoulders. I clung to him, needing his warmth and his loving. He threw my shirt aside and gently caressed my breasts over my bra, all the while staring deep into my eyes. He stood, took off his shirt and shoes and opened the button fly of his jeans..

A field came into view. Grass growing lushly and plentiful. A beautiful summer's twilight. Free, my arms outstretched as I ran in a flowing white gown that trailed behind me. Off in the distance the forest was my goal. Twirling, spinning, flying.

Finally, the woods. A clearing to sit down in and catch my breath. I laid upon the bed of leaves facing the stars that were magically appearing in the sky. Woosh, a strong wind and HE appeared. Without a word HE came to me. Hurriedly brushing his long hair aside, he took me roughly into HIS arms and kissed me deeply. HE took my face into HIS hands, staring at me as if HE longed to tell me something. The wind blew across HIS face as HE threw HIS head back and silently cried out my name.

Part Two
Chapter 22
The Eversod

The Master

"Sire?"

"Yes, Vincent?"

"May I?"

"Yes, come."

Vincent materialized in the chamber to find HIM, in HIS throne. HE turned to face Vincent.

"What is it?"

The room was bare but for softly draped white fabric. Golden leaves held back the chiffon to form soft folds and a gentle breeze caused the fabric to bellow.

"Sire, it is time for the tour."

"Is it that time already?"

"Yes Sire."

The breeze died as HE got up to accompany Vincent. They exited the chamber and walked together down a long hallway where a man sat. The man was a well-known revolutionist on earth and therefore HE wanted to personally introduce him into the workings of The Moderation Rooms.

"Mr. Jones, I have the honor to present —"

"Please, Vincent allow me — Hello Mr. Jones, I am your new taskmaster, or shall I say, your new boss. I would like to show you around your new home. So, if you will just follow Vincent and myself, we will begin in The Moderation Rooms."

Alan Jones rose and followed them.

Taking the lead, HE spoke.

"Mr. Jones you are now in operation headquarters. This is our, how shall I put it? Our executive suite level. We will be taking you to The Moderation Rooms as we call them as that WILL be your main responsibility...to oversee a portion of them.

Come, Mr. Jones, you seem to be lagging a bit. Don't get over-whelmed yet, for you will have plenty of time to get used to our world."

They proceeded down a brightly lit round white hallway.

"Over here on the walls you will find portraits of some of our more famous employees. For example, here we have AW as we affectionately call him.... We all were surprised to see him here, myself included. He, by the way, is situated with his own office off-site. And here we have JK, who has since moved back up-stairs. Johnny prefers the lighter side, ahhhhhhh, but to each his own. Oh, and of course, we have Adolph. He genuinely was a bad seed, so he now works in the basement, and I'm embarrassed to admit that he likes it. No sleep for the wicked, as they say.

"You may be wondering at this point WHAT THE FUCK IS GO-ING ON? Well, Mr. Jones I will tell you what the fuck is going on, so you may relax and let the wind out of your fat belly. Step this way, Mr. Jones we must descend to the lower level."

Vincent opened the elevator gates and pulled the elevator doors closed and pressed the button marked "B".

"Your feeble mind may not at this point have grasped that you have died, 'passed away' or as I explain to all our new employees, you have come to the place that you always truly believed you would.

186

Oh, Mr. Jones, don't look so surprised, and please don't look so scared."

They stepped out of the elevator and went down another long, brightly lit rounded white hallway but with no paintings on the wall.

"This is not HELL. Is it Vincent?" HE said, laughing.

"I am not THE DEVIL. And you are not condemned to damnation for all eternity. This is only, Vincent, what would you call it? It just is as I've said, the place that you always truly believed you would come to after you died. We have such a flourishing community simply because so many believe the same scenario, so many sad souls that never considered the possibilities, but I digress...Let me backtrack to the beginning.

"When a mortal lives, he believes. And he has certain beliefs of what will happen and where he will go after his earthly duty is done, after he dies. Whatever it is that lies deep, and my friend, I mean deep, within his soul, is actually what happens. Forget what he may preach, or what charity he sings for, the only thing that counts is what lies buried within his soul.

"Young children ascend immediately. Yet what about religion, you may ask? Religion is complicated and may be considered by many to be a cult. There are many religions with many beliefs, for example Judaism does not have much dogma about the afterlife, but it is common for a Jew to believe in a place similar to the Christian heaven. Martyrs believe that they will spend their afterlife with 72 dark-eyed virgins in paradise, but this paradise may be somewhat limited from what I understand due to the tragedy they incur and the guilt deeply buried associated with it. Some do come here. Death in Hinduism is very spiritual, and they strongly believe in the rebirth and reincarnation of souls. These souls bounce back to earth immediately into a new life, sometimes as animals. And so on, and so forth.

"There are, of course, many who just, poooooof, become dark matter because they had no thought–they never considered the next life, they put off thinking about it until it was too late, they did not deserve an afterlife. And, there are those who dreamed of traveling to far off planets who find themselves in colonies of like-minded individuals. There are, my friend, parallel universes where these space travelers attempt to go, but I hear the worm holes are quite challenging. You may at a future date ascend to the higher place; trust me though, it's more interesting down here, but that's just my humble opinion.

"So many earthlings are convinced that there is only heaven and hell. I tell you, more wind up here than you would think. Here is The Eversod, The Moderation Rooms. The place where the souls who had a bit of an imagination come. The place that these confused souls belong. As you were taught in school, matter can neither be created nor destroyed, therefore their soul energy becomes part of our community."

They began walking quickly.

"So, my friend Mr. Jones, just as in any corporation in this dawn of the twenty first century, we do have to keep up with the Jones'. Ha! The matter of human souls is dealt with logically."

They resumed walking down the hall.

"This is a corporation you are entering. We have a product that needs to be distributed and contained."

He stopped in his path and turned to face Jones.

"Our product, Mr. Jones, is Evil."

Mr. Jones stood frozen under his stare.

"Mystery, heartache, disease, despair, despondency, depression, destruction, my, what a mouthful. These terrible afflictions of humanity need to be controlled and monitored."

They continued walking.

"Think of it this way, Mr. Jones, if there was no sorrow, there would be no happiness, if there was no low, there could be no high, E=MC2, everything IS relative, do you understand?

There always has been and there always will be, and there always must be a balance.

So, in keeping with this logic, if there is a need for 'The Evil Side' this Evil Side must be maintained and monitored and controlled in an orderly manner.

Evil cannot, nor will not ever run rampant amongst mankind, although mortals may not see it this way.

That's OK, Vincent, I know I get carried away on this point, thank you, I'm fine.

I will continue.

"That starving child in Indonesia, that injured soldier lying in pain in Bosnia, every heartsick adolescent in agony over her boyfriend, each poor Joe depressed about his lousy raise, they are, each and every one of them entered, logged, noted, recorded into our computers in The Moderation Rooms—"

He stopped at the end of the hallway in front of two large metal doors.

He lifted his finger and the doors slowly parted to reveal a room so vast that the back wall looked to be on the horizon. There were rows upon rows, as far as the eye could see, of computer workstations, each with an operator at the helm.

Mr. Jones stared in awe at the sight.

The room was dimly lit and in the center was a large revolving electric globe hanging in suspension below the ceiling, turning in a clockwise direction. Red lights flashed on it in a seemingly meaningless manner. A center aisle divided the room in half. He led the way down this aisle.

"To the left we deal with the Eastern hemisphere and to the right, the Western. Notice we have a special section for the Middle East, which has always been a problem. Also notice that the computer system that we utilize is a combination between MacIntosh and IBM, the best of both worlds, so to say. We are all connected through an Internet very similar to the World Wide Web that has become so popular as of late with earthlings, but of course, it is a much more advanced system here. Each part of the world is divided regionally. Each operator you see is in charge of a different portion of the population and the assignments are rotated regularly. No two operators are monitoring the individuals of a same family. That is done so as to avoid any conflicts, and to ensure that each individual gets fair treatment.

"I see that you are listening closely, Mr. Jones, that is good. A fascinating place we have here, wouldn't you say?

Where was I? Oh, yes, let us step closer and I will briefly explain how this works. You will, of course, receive a formal training, but I am feeling verbose, come."

They walked over to one of the operators.

"Mr. Jones this is Ms. Savintino, and she is currently in charge of Southern Miami.

If you look closely you will see that there is an information bar across the top."

He pressed the bar.

A monitor grew from the computer virtually, taking up 20 feet before them.

"This area gives us specific details about any one particular individual."

"Mikey Beltrain."

Mikey walked down the street. Cuban by birth, American by immigration, age 33, 5'11", dark hair, darker brown eyes. A small black derby perched on his head, steel gray button down short sleeve shirt caressed his biceps and fell over well-fitting dark jeans. He smoked a cigarette with his left hand and walked with a purpose.

He moved to the beat of his iPod that was situated in his jeans front pocket. JT sang through his earbuds. He was very happy, and his body language spoke clearly of his pleasure. The daylight was fading. He walked. The neon lights in the stores along Collins Avenue were coming alive, T-Shirts sang to the tourists and hotel-front fountains aglow in colored lights lit up the boulevard against the pythalo blue sky. He stopped at the corner, the store across the street. He picked out daffodils because she had once told him that daffodils made her happy and this made him smile. Everything about Eve made him smile. She was The One for him and the day that he got down on one knee was approaching quickly.

Eve was expecting him for an early dinner and they were planning on a lazy Friday night in front of cable TV. Planning....they had lots of plans. They were planning to get engaged, they were planning to move to the suburbs of Tampa where they would have 2.5 children, a dog, and a house with a backyard.

He got to the corner of Collins and Miami Blvd. and made a quick left. His heart began beating faster when he thought of Eve and how soon she would be in his arms. Her smile and her almond shaped eyes drove him crazy. She was his and that made him even more crazy.

He stepped into the gutter, taking a glance at his watch, and as he lifted his head a car came barreling around the corner from his left. BAM. The daffodils exploded. He flew 20 feet into the air. When he reached the ground, the forces involved in the accident made his shoes fly off as they often do simply because his shoelaces were not tied tightly enough to keep them on. His neck was broken in two places, his broken rib had pierced his spleen and he had died upon impact to the ground. This was not included in his plans.

In the second before he died his life flashed before him, but not from the beginning to the present, as most people think. One's life flashes forward on the moment before death showing where one's soul energy will go when death is finally upon them. A pulse, and an exchange of energy showed in the center of the screen and the monitor collapsed on itself and back into the computer.

"He is now one of our members, such as yourself. He is currently in the introduction seminar area and in time he too may choose to stay, to descend, to ascend or to disappear into space's dark matter."Our world here exists to house the souls that come to this realm and to monitor the level of sorrow, that the individuals on earth will experience in their lifetime. One mortal's sorrow is divided between another mortal's sorrow upon earth with an algorithm. The information is generated from here in The Eversod but the bottom line is determined from information received from Him, up above. Ultimately He is the Boss."

He pointed upwards. "Prayers do work, and miracles do occur. These anomalies are out of our control.

We do work together, you see, He and I. He bases his findings as to how much sorrow we are to distribute. He has his own reasons. You will learn the subtleties of your duties in due time. And on that note, I will leave you with Vincent who will complete the tour. I am suddenly weary of this and shall be on my way. Good day, Mr. Jones, and good luck to you."

He disappeared before Alan Jones could blink his eyes.

Chapter 23
The Eversod

Spring

Seasons in The Eversod lasted for the human equivalent of years, decades, although they did follow the natural path of winter, spring, summer and fall as on earth. It could be harsh existing within these constraints, yearning for change. Court was held in all four seasons, the winter court being the most popular amongst the members– to gather for heat in the frigid cold. Seasons were true, and winters could be very difficult, with summers being brutally hot. Work was maintained on a 9-5 basis, this method having been adopted many years ago to reflect the modern mode. Those from the renaissance had found this an ease from the 12-hour work days of times past. Classes were conducted for all new members in the mechanics of the software currently being used in The Moderation Rooms. Dorms speckled the countryside in shapes of castles, mansions, and houses. The Eversod was infinite, and no one could die, only exist as they were when they became members.

She sat alone on a stone bench in the courtyard, her face turned up to the springtime sun. She had opened the neckline of her gown to better feel the warmth. The never-ending winter had thankfully let go of its grip upon the land. This was her favorite time of the long seasons, the eternally long seasons. The birds sang gleefully to each other and the leaves of the trees had taken their sweet time to blossom into green. Members took advantage of the beautiful weather and tried to spend as much time outdoors when they were not working in The Moderation Rooms. Dressed in the notion of where and when they passed, the members were quite a site of variety. A mixture in time. Love existed in The Eversod. A man from the renaissance finding himself loving a woman from the 1920s was very common, as much as were members enamored of those from the same domain. Weddings came to pass as the need for companionship was crucial, although no "human" children could be conceived in this realm. Many weddings occurred in the spring, more so than any other time of year.

She alone was the anomaly, having been born into The Eversod. Her parents had lived in this world long before any of the laws of nature had taken effect. HE knew that HE had a precious treasure with HIS Woman.

She daydreamed of what she could do to improve the lives of the members that were under HIS control. A purpose was simply so important to her. To exist here in The Eversod with no other meaning than to please HIM was not a reality that she was willing to accept. Her royal status inspired her to make a difference. She COULD make a change, she COULD work toward a better more meaningful existence here, she COULD find a way to make eternity more bearable. She knew this, but only how to make it happen was the question.

She felt HIM approaching.

"My love, I have been looking for you."

"And, so, you have found me," she said.

"Are you enjoying your sunbath?" HE bent down to kiss her.

"Why, yes, I am."

"Do you mind if I join you?"

HE sat down next to her and adjusted his neckline as she had done.

"Finally, we have spring," HE said.

"Yes, just in time for some change."

"Change?" HE said.

"Yes, change – we have 122 members wedding this season."

"Do we?" HE said.

"I think we need to relieve them of their duties for a time for a celebration and to make this a reoccurring practice."

"No," HE said, still facing the sun.

"No?" she said, sitting up.

"No, this can only lead to a bad precedent. I don't think this is a good idea." HE remained leaning back.

She sat back against the bench.

"But..."

"No."

"This will lead to good relations within our Eversod," she said.

"I think not, do not worry yourself about good relations."

"What shall I worry myself about?" she said.

"Me."

Chapter 24
The Eversod

Summer

Spring changed gradually into summer. The leaves on the trees burned from the long time of sun upon them. Birds flew slowly across the bright blue skies as if in a daze, searching for water. The hot winds blew across the lands and the members took refuge in the working of The Moderation Rooms, which were cool and soothing.

Cassendre walked the halls of the Castle in a light blue gown, light and cool. Thinking of how to ease the lives of the members in the terrible heat of summer, to make a change in their existence, she approached the Chamber.

The doors opened upon her approach.

"Ah, my love!" HE said.

"I know you were not expecting me," she said.

"Always my pleasure." HE took her right hand and kissed it while looking into her eyes.

The Chamber was cold, almost uncomfortably cold. The walls were colored a pale green. Softly blowing drapery of beads, iridescent, hung from opposite areas. Matching pillows placed meticulously followed the curve of the room with a large rug that looked like a moving ocean taking up most of the floor. Although the Chamber was cold the everlasting fireplace burned brightly.

"My, it is so hot." She took up a gather of feathers from the shelf and began fanning herself with them.

"I take it that you are cool and comfortable within the castle," he said.

"Yes, but the members are not so fortunate."

"No? The Moderation Rooms are quite comfortable," HE said.

"Yes, but the ones not working at this time are not. Possibly can we open the pools on the west side for the members to swim and relieve themselves? They have all been humans, they deserve this. Their wants and needs count."

"No."

"But why?"

"The pools have not been opened for many years and would require much construction."

"Why not start the construction now for summers to come?" she asked.

"Because that would need years of development, which would take away time from The Moderation Rooms."

"But..."

"No."

"This will lead to good relations within our Eversod," she said.

"The answer is no. Do not worry yourself about theses good relations," HE said. "Worry yourself about me."

Suddenly she had an idea that she should worry herself about. "But I must make my approach with time," she thought.

Chapter 25
The Eversod

Fall

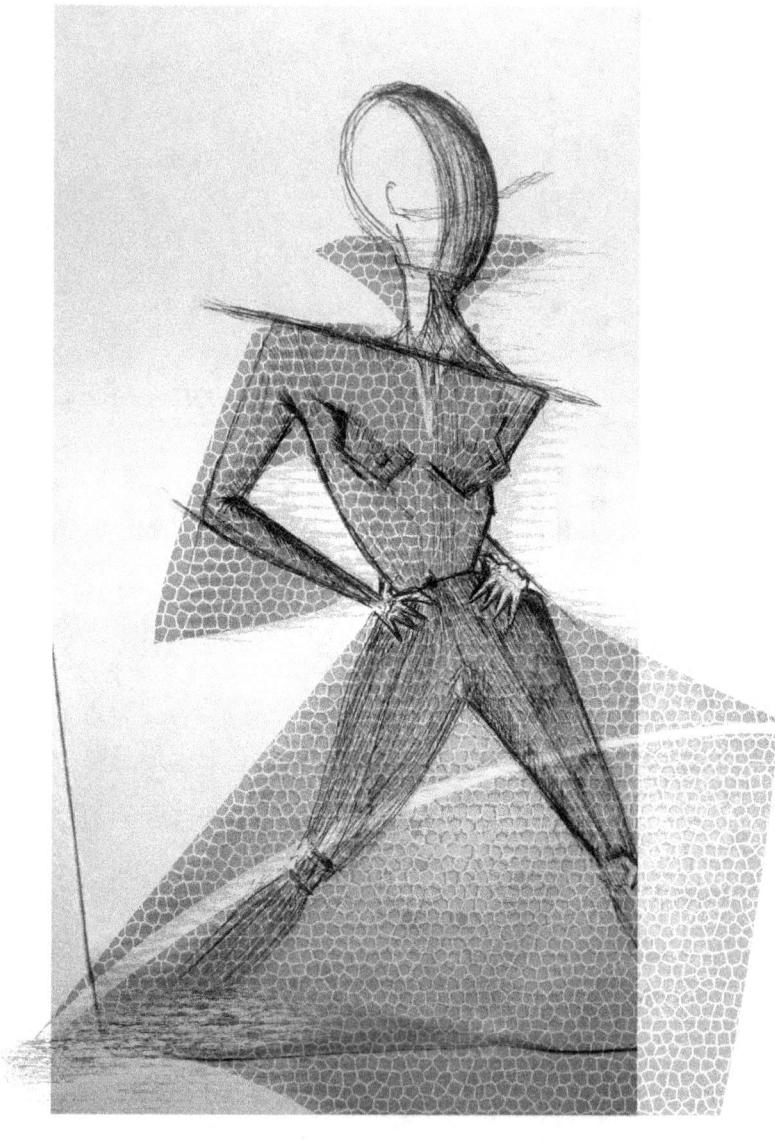

"Cassendre! Are you ready? Come now, let's go."

She appeared from the dressing room adjusting her earring and taking off the diamond crown that sat on her head. She placed it on the shelf. She was dressed in a rich long-sleeved orange gown that had a hood which reached the small of her back; it was the color of the leaves that they were going to visit. Her long dark hair was held partially in the back of her head with an ebony clip.

"Is your crown too heavy for you, my love?"

"Yes, too much for a relaxing day in the country."

"Are you ready? I am anxious to spend the day with you."

"I am now." She stood on tip-toe and kissed HIM on the nose. "Bo, come!"

The yellow Labrador joined them.

"Lady, come!" HE snapped his fingers – a female yellow Labrador appeared and Cassendre laughed.

"Ahhhhhhh, now we are complete!"

"Yes," HE said.

HE circled his arm above the small group and pointed up in one movement.

They appeared on a hillside. The day was a beautiful autumn

day; bright sunlight toyed with white intermittent clouds. A chill was in the air, but it was warmed by the sunshine. The rolling grass showed no sign of turning brown–that was to occur in the long winter to come. Tree after tree in the distance glowed with the brilliant colors of the season, orange and crimson and gold and green. HE lifted his hand and a group of these mystifying trees arranged themselves in a broad circle around them. The dogs frolicked, playing together and running, never straying too far.

"Ohhh, BEAUTIFUL!" She clapped her hand, turning in circles to take in the spectacle that HE had presented to her. The dogs joined in the fun, chasing her long skirts, and then resumed their play.

"Cassendre, step back." HE pointed at her.

She took a step back and her orange gown turned to shimmering gold. She laughed out loud, turning about, bringing the hood about her and twirling her long skirts. The gown then turned to a glimmering crimson. She continued to show her pleasure as her gown changed color in turn to the varied colors of the leaves surrounding them.

"Ahhhhhh, delicious!" She threw her arms around HIM, kissing HIM passionately and then HE laughed.

"Cassendre, sit with me."

HE spread HIS arm, and a red blanket arranged itself on the ground. A carafe of red wine and two goblets were situated in the center.

They sat on the blanket.

HE poured them each a glass of wine and they made a toast.

"Lemniscate."

"Lemniscate. Eternity." They sipped the wine.

"Eternity is a long time," she said. "The first time I discovered eternity was at the feet of my father when he asked me if I could contemplate forever – living forever."

"What did you tell him?"

"Well, after thinking about it for a few days, I told him that I was not so sure that I wanted to be a part of this eternity idea. Eternity was indeed a very long time."

She lay down on her back.

"What can I do for you my love?" HE leaned over her.

"Do for me? I'm not sure there is anything you don't do for me."

"I want to please you, keep you happy," HE said.

"It is I who should want to please YOU!"

"But you do."

"This life we lead is idyllic. You truly try so hard and that is...." She sat up on her elbow, "either wonderful beyond words or a nightmare waiting to happen."

"Really," HE said. "For you are mine my dear, and if anything that is mine is so unhappy to call what we have a nightmare, that would make ME very unhappy."

"There is no nightmare, I am sorry that I said that – I am yours – yes, I suppose I am yours, but what has happened to me?"

They returned to the chamber later that day.

The chamber was decorated in the colors that they had experienced that afternoon.

Rich amber lighting, light shades of green and brown.

A large log laying before the fireplace and gold shimmering curtains framed the sides of the area.

He turned the fire up having checked the hearth.

Bo was sent to settle in on his cushioned bed, the female dog, Lady was gone, back to her residence.

Cassendre paced slowly in front of the fire and HE sat reclined on HIS throne.

My love, thank you for a wonderful day," she said.

She approached HIM and kissed HIM, holding HIS face.

"My pleasure, Cassendre."

"The colors of the trees are so majestic, I do not look forward to the winter to come."

"No fear, I will keep you warm."

She moved toward HIM.

"So, Vincent tells me that we are approaching a record number of members in the working of our Moderation Rooms."

"Vincent has a large mouth – that should be noted," HE said.

"Vincent says that belief amongst mankind is at a low."

"Vincent should keep his opinions to himself," HE said.

"Vincen—"

He stepped up behind her and took her jaw into his hand, lovingly yet strongly stroking it.

"I see no reason for you to have such an interest in what Vincent says."

"But, I–"

"Do as you're told."

He let go of the grasp he had on her.

"I'm weary from our day. I'm going to lie down." She exited from his view to the bed within the chamber and picked up the book that she had been reading, *Stories from The World*, losing herself within the words and pictures. She turned the pages; images of earth filled her vision. Soon she found herself drifting off and dreaming of earthly regions, lakes, oceans, and clouds.

Dressed in black pants, black riding boots, a black turtle neck sweater, and a black leather jacket, she descended from the white clouds surrounding her to an Irish pub. The facade included emerald green window sills and an oversized emerald green arch. She looked around the empty street and opened the front door. A machine playing music stood in the corner. A large withered bar circled the back wall with an older looking man, gray beard, behind it. Patrons sat about, drinking pints of beer, singing along to the "Victory of Connor O'Colin." As she entered, the door slammed behind her and everyone in the bar froze and turned to look at her, drinks still in hand. The clock on the far wall stopped, a rat ran across the wet wood, and the glass in the barkeep's hand fell to the floor and shattered. Startled, she smiled, and they then resumed their antics. She approached the bar and asked for an ale.

"Hi, darlin' what kind of ale might that be?" the barkeeper said in a heavy brogue.

"An amber please."

He turned to the tap and presented her with an amber ale.

"Thank you," she said.

"Can you kindly tell me what year this is and where exactly I am?"

"Ahhh, you're one of those, I should have known, we get them sometimes, the time travelers. You be in Belfast in the year 1935. Belfast is the capital and largest city of Northern Ireland. Our beautiful establishment has been here since 1711, and if I may say you're very welcome here, pretty lady."

He smiled exposed his missing front tooth.

"Is something happening here? I sense a feeling of excitement."

"Well, what you might be talking of is that last week workmen in County Clare unearthed a statue of Jesus during excavations for road making. It looks to be a grand celebration."

"Humans seem to love this Jesus."

"Well not all of us, but a good many of us."

"Do you like being human?" she asked.

He laughed.

"What do you mean darlin', what else shall I be?"

Be

Be

Be

The bar started turning, faster and faster and disappeared.

She found herself dressed in a white hooded cloth robe, held closed with a gold rope She looked around and saw a large old stone wall. Men in black hats with curls cascading from their temples in black suits, white striped shawls with long strings adorning their shoulders. They hovered near the wall and bent methodically in what looked like prayer. The spirituality surrounding the area was palatable. The women accompanying them wore dresses and wigs. She walked closer to the wall. The sun was shining brightly, and the temperature was very warm. Wondering what they were doing, she approached a friendly looking young man.

"Can you kindly tell me what is going on here?"

"How can you be here and not know?" he answered.

"This is the Wailing Wall – an ancient limestone wall in the Old City of Jerusalem, a relatively small remaining segment of a far longer ancient wall known as the Western Wall. We place notes into the cracks of the Wailing Wall containing written prayers to God. We pray to God."

"Who is your God that you write letters to? Is it Jesus?"

He looked at her with an incredulous stare.

"Can you kindly tell me what year this is and if you like being human?" she said.

He screamed, "Are you crazy? Eric, Razi, Joseph, come here, this woman is a devil, come here, help me."

Help me

Help me

Help me

The blocks of the wall dismantled and turned in circles, her robe wound around her with the gold rope reaching toward the sky and all disappeared.

She looked around and found herself on a beautiful beach dressed in a black string bikini.

There were no clouds in the sky; a hot sun beat down upon the shore. She started walking down the empty beach. On the water were mechanical machines that held seats, brightly colored with a sleek design. The ocean gently lapped onto the sand.

As she walked, she sensed someone walking behind her.

A tall dark man with dreadlocks approached her.

She turned, not afraid.

"Hello," she said.

"Ire! And, hello to you. Would you like to smoke with me?"

"Smoke what?" she said.

He laughed.

"You're in Jamaica, my friend. There's only one thing to smoke."

"Okay," she said.

He took out a small plastic bag and a piece of paper and did something fancy. He lit the thing with a fancy light of fire. He took a toke and passed it to her.

She took a drag.

They both looked out at the beautiful ocean.

"Thank you," she said.

"More life more strength."

"What a beautiful place," she said.

"To di worl!"

"Can you kindly tell me what year this is?"

"Oh, honey, you must be wacked."

"Wacked?"

"Yes, stoned."

"Do you like being human?"

"Oh, my darlin' what is the alternative?"

He smiled broadly, his two front gold teeth shining off of the sun.

The beach and the sky became one and turned into an ice cream cone.

She found herself in New Jersey, across the street from city hall and the local police department. Dressed in jeans, small work boots and a tank top, she parked her car. Using her door key, she balanced coffees and her banana and stomped up the stairs.

"Shiloh! Hi Christine, good morning Frank, hey Peter, what's up Deb? Where is Joe? Hello darling – Olivia, here's coffee."

She entered her office and instinctually turned on the computer on her desk.

"Olivia, I have to ask you something," she said to the office next door.

"Not now, busy, busy, busy."

"Okay."

She went into the kitchen and cracked open a hard-boiled egg, cut it into pieces, added salt and pepper, and ate it slowly.

"Olivia, I have to ask you something."

"Not now, busy, busy, busy."

She checked into her computer – the screen saver going crazy – Manny chasing Doodle.

Oh, my.

"Olivia, I have to ask you something," she said.

"Give me a minute, busy, busy, busy."

She checked her email and walked into Olivia's office.

Olivia sat glued to the computer on her desk, the coffee she had brought her centered between her hands. Olivia wore a blouse, cut out on the shoulders, and copper laden gloves with the forefingers missing. Her long curly hair colored in shades of red surrounded her face. Three tattoos on the underside of her forearms were showing.

"Can you kindly tell me what year this is?"

"Oh, darling..." she replied without a glance.

"Do you like being human?"

Olivia stopped what she was doing, looked at her, smiled broadly and said, "Honey, I'm not human."

Not human.

Not human.

Not human.

The office twirled around and around and around and disappeared.

Cassendre moaned in her sleep, softly moving. HE approached the bed, laid down next to her, and took her into HIS arms as she dreamt, caressing her body gently. She smiled in her sleep and moved closer to HIM. HE reached to the front of her gown and tugged gently on the lace cord that held it in place. Her breasts settled against the fabric that had been liberated. HE rose on his elbow and reached in to take her breasts in HIS hand. HIS fingers covered her nipples and squeezed gently. Then again, not so gently. She moaned and turned to face HIM. HE reached down and lifted her gown. HE slipped HIS center finger into her, deep. Looking into her eyes. Harder HE moved HIS finger and then took HIS forefinger to caress the essence that was her. Was her, again and again, and she cried out, Ahhhhhhhhhh, and laughed and moved close to HIM again on her side.

They laid like that for hours.

Chapter 26
The Eversod

Winter

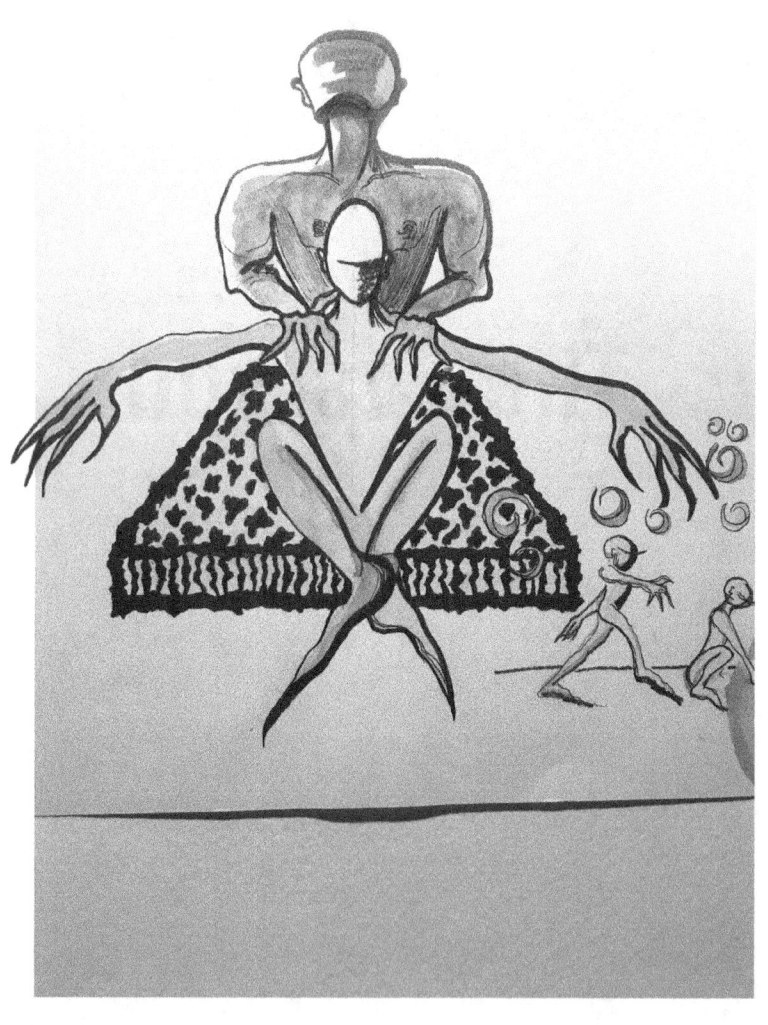

The large stone quad was buzzing with energy. This was the Winter Court. Members were milling about discussing, quarreling, and petting their dogs. Dogs were a common site in The Eversod, having such a deep connection to mankind. Members who had owned dogs on earth now owned them here.

The Moderation Band was preparing for the Winter Court Gathering. The stage was being set. The electric guitars were being tuned. The bass players were checking their notes. The drummer and the bongo player were conferring. Behind the band set-up was a mesh fabric decoration spanning the stage from left to right, up and down–uplit and casting deep shadows of indigo blue against the velvet backdrop.

A bell chimed, the musicians took their instruments and their places, and the members took their seats.

HE and Cassendre entered the auditorium. The members stood up, clapping, screaming for them. HE and Cassendre moved to the front seats and sat. The auditorium became silent and HE stood up facing the assemblage.

"Members of The Eversod."

"Work is something we think will one day go far away, but in reality it never does. We must, all of us, learn to embrace the working of The Moderation Rooms and hold the mechanisms dear to our hearts."

"For this Winter Season Court Gathering, I welcome you, beseech you, and command you to forget your day, your toil, and hard work and join my Cassendre and I in the indulgence of The Moderation Band."

The members went wild with applause. HE sat and the lights adjusted.

Acoustic guitars, four, in unison began. Bass in a tantric pattern began. Classical string instruments and the drums began. And began. And began. Harmonic and melodic music sprang forth. An organ played off stage and out of sight. Five robed women joined from stage right, singing staccato, arms stretched up to the high, tall vaulted ceilings. In the back of the stage the mesh fabric moved in a wave motion. The dark shadows of the open weave fabric moved with the bass and the lights pulsated softly.

The members went wild with appreciation.

"Come in, Vincent."

The oak door opened and revealed Vincent standing there. He walked into the chamber. It was blue. Sky blue. White snakeskins were thrown about like an afterthought and a sixteenth century fainting couch upholstered in white ticking was pushed to the right side of the room. Tinted blueberry blue fur rugs laid on the floor. Vincent smiled inwardly. His Master was looking brilliant with energy as always.

"There is a disturbance. I feel it. Tell me what is happening," HE said.

"Boston, USA – the year 2013, Sire. Two youths have upended earth. They have set off two bombs on a celebratory day for the region. It has caused deaths, injuries and unspeakable devastation to the lower extremities of many innocent bystanders. One of the suspects is dead. He went directly down. I checked earlier. The other one is 19 years of age and if put to death may come our way."

"I want to be alerted if he is to join our membership. This is an exceptional case."

HIS day began with a run of the dogs, Bowie, HIS dog accompanied HIM back to the chamber. Alone with the dog HE spoke to him.

"Sit, Bo. Good boy, Bo, wasn't that fun running on the hillside with your friends, now go settle down in your corner while I re-adjust."

The chamber spun, the gold bead trimmings came into place magically from the high ceiling. HE smiled at the dog and flicked HIS finger west as the fire came into being. Hmmmm, we need some red, HE thought and turned quickly. The walls moved in a clockwise direction and brick after brick took its position on the round facade one by one. Quickly the centrifugal motion slowed and came to a stop.

The chamber, HIS doing, HIS creation as always. HE fancied himself a master of design and proved it over and over by re-creating HIS environment every day. It gave HIM pleasure. The round room held fire – a large fireplace made of smooth onyx and black marble, glowing with a roaring inferno that shed the only light. Bright gold pillows were now strewn about–sheer gold shimmering fabric hung from the rafters and moved carelessly as if breathing. Her golden throne resided next to HIS. HE covered it in rich brocade fabrics made of tones of yellow ochre and earth.

HIS throne never changed.

At the south side, a large bed with posts made of stone sat covered with cushions of silk, sheets of satin. HE altered the colors to black and crimson and orange and yellow and deep brown and cream.

HE stood back and observed his handiwork. Hmmmmm, a tall vase made of crystal appeared next to the bed and suddenly filled with dozens of long stemmed roses, blood roses, thorns, and leaves. Happy now, HE turned up the inferno just a notch and smiled to HIMSELF.

There was a knock at the oak door.

"Vincent, come!"

Vincent walked in, standing tall and bowed. "Sire. An update for you."

The breeze in the room took Vincent's long blonde hair in various directions. His black suit hung perfectly on his large frame. A pure white shirt accompanied by a dark magenta and pale blue silk tie masterfully woven into a windsor knot complimented his coloring and his blue eyes. He stood straight, the first lieutenant that he was – the large yellow lab greeted him by smelling his feet.

"Be gone, Bowie," HE said.

Bowie stepped away, looking behind him with a half snarl on his snout and retreated to his bed.

"Show me, how does our corporation fair?"

HE took a step backward, reached forward with both of HIS hands grabbing the air in front of HIM, and pulled back HIS hands toward HIM then letting go with wide fingers. A large thin pane of clear glass, rounded corners appeared between them. In the center a mass of green color spread about, small red lights populated the perimeter. The reds and yellows of the fire behind him were gently reflected in the glass.

From Vincent's point of view the green mass had formed into a world map spread from east to west.

HE stood with his hands clasped behind HIS back, legs spread slightly, watching intently, HIS head bowed slightly, eyes looking out from beneath HIS dark brows. HIS point of view showed the green mass had also formed into the world map viewable from east to west.

"You are already aware of Bosnia," Vincent said.

Vincent touched Bosnia on the map and almost the whole of the country lit up with the red lights.

HE observed the red blinking lights.

"The civil war in Afghanistan beginning in 1996 will be bringing a large influx of members."

Vincent touched the glass where Afghanistan was, and red lights began to blink in that area.

"The 1998 Kosovo War is small but significant."

He touched the map and red lights blinked in Kosovo.

"The year 2016 is still relatively peaceful, although I have met with the leaders of 2017. A major conflict will be coming our way in that year with what could be massive causalities. Although I cannot predict The Third World War as of yet, hopefully it will not come to pass. Many of those lost in 2027 are equally lost in their faith, they are floundering and will be joining us.

"We have gotten notification from above about the overload of new initiates that will be on the way. As you know that is as far a spanse at a time as HE above will allow us to travel as of now. The troops are ready as always, The Moderation Rooms are primed for expansion and unfortunately for those on earth, we are prepared."

"Well then thank you, Vincent. Please let me know when the next dignitary joins us so that I may greet them myself."

"Yes Sire."

HE raised his arms to the glass, taking it and crushing it as a piece of paper until it disappeared.

Cassendre found herself circling the cold perimeter of the castle, walking quickly. It was late in the day and the sun was beginning to set. Her thoughts were in a turmoil as she spoke aloud to herself.

"Oh!" She pulled her hair back away from her head.

"I must find a way."

"This is so very important to me, I must find a way. So stubborn HE is I must insist."

"How am I GOING TO MAKE THIS HAPPEN? How am I going to convince HIM to allow this? HE will never allow this. I must make HIM see things my way. If I have to beg or plead or bang my head against his GOD FORSAKEN MANTLE, I will not stop until I HAVE MY WAY. MY WAY, MY WAY is the ONLY WAY that I will ACCEPT. I will promise HIM anything, agree to whatever HE comes up with. I have contemplated this for so long, it is the perfect time. But I must be clever in my approach."

The oak door opened.

Cassendre entered and walked into the chamber, her plum colored gown, long to the floor was clasped at the right shoulder, flowing softly about her. Her beauty took HIS breath away.

"Vincent, perfect as always," she said to the first lieutenant.

"M'lady," he bowed.

"A pleasure to have you in my presence." She smiled and clapped her hands for the dog.

"Bo! Come!"

The dog came to her with an equally large smile on his face, his tail wagging and ears alert.

"Vincent, you may leave us now," HE said and pointed at Vincent.

Vincent disappeared in a puff of smoke.

She laughed.

"You make me laugh when you do that!"

"The better to please you, my dear." HE joined in her laughter.

HE sat down on his throne, facing the fire.

She loosened the diamond crown from her head and threw it to the floor. It slid along the black granite, coming to rest at the edge of the rug near the hearth of the fire. The dog looked up at her, licked her finger, then went to his bed in the far corner of the room crossing his front paws, settling in.

HE turned to look at what she had thrown down.

HE rose, taking her right hand and bringing it to his lips.

"What, my love, are diamonds not for you? Shall I get you rubies or emeralds?"

She smiled, her hazel eyes twinkling, her long black hair glowing from the fire.

"No, I want only abalone shells." She laughed and pulled her hand back from his touch and stepped forward, holding her hands to the fire.

"But abalone shells could never complement your beauty the way that diamonds do," HE said.

She turned to face HIM.

"And no one can ever create a fire the way that you do, my love, you're very good at it." She laughed again.

"Where have you been?" HE asked.

She stepped around HIM and went to the carafe of wine on the cupboard next to the wall.

"Oh, here and there."

"Here and there?"

"Yes, here and there." She poured HIM a glass of wine and handed it to HIM.

"And you choose not to be more specific?"

She poured herself a glass of the wine.

"Yes, that is my choice, my free will, not to be more specific, you don't like this, do you?"

She held her glass up in a toast.

"Let's make a deal."

"What kind of deal?"

"I do as I do, and you don't question it."

HE lowered his glass as well as HIS eyebrows.

"Really. I can't imagine what has brought this on." HE placed the glass of wine on the side bar without taking a sip.

"You, you don't realize, I will love you till the end of time, but I need ME. YOU know, you treat me at times as a possession, as that diamond crown that sits upon my head.

I am bored, BORED, BORED, BORED of this life, of perfection that we lead. I am tired of court, of the fields, of the lords and ladies, the biker chicks and hoodlums, the members, The Moderation Rooms, even of Vincent, I am tired of this CHAMBER, no matter how much you change it. I want a child but you, the MASTER cannot give me one because of your dealings with Him above. All I find is that I live to listen to you, I live to please you, YOU are my child.

I don't want to feel level, I want to FEEL MY EMOTIONS, to FEEL PASSIONATE IN A NEW AND EXCITING WAY. To have highs and lows and NOT JUST PERFECTION.

I am ME with wants and needs that you don't seem to care about."

"CARE ABOUT?! HE screamed. "I WOULD KILL FOR YOU, I LIVE FOR YOU, I WOULD DIE FOR YOU!"

"AND I YOU – SO MAKE A DEAL WITH ME," she screamed back.

"You realize what you're saying? Is this a WAGER?"

"Not exactly."

"Deals come with rules, love," HE said.

She placed her glass down without having taken a sip.

HE started pacing around the chamber.

HE stopped in front of her and took a deep breath.

"What is it exactly that you want?"

She walked to the center of the chamber, her back to him. She raised her head, speaking softly and slowly.

"I want, I need, I require – how can I say it? space...time... time to use MY brain, MY rhythm, MY logic, to come out from under your wing and explore, to have MY life count–to experience adventure, and yes, to maybe fail, but then to rise again. To be happy on my own, to be strong."

She turned to him.

"TO BE human," she decreed.

"Do you mean what you're saying? Do you not love me and our life together? Do you want to forsake all that we have?"

"For a spell – we have forever, don't we? The longevity and depth of our relationship is so intense, what can possibly destroy it? A short separation? A mortal lifetime?"

She flicked her finger.

"Ahhhh, the mere beat of a butterfly's wing...please, do this for me, trust me, trust us."

"I repeat, every deal comes with rules, love," HE said.

"What are your rules?"

HE ran HIS hands through HIS black hair.

"Cassendre, please don't make me do this."

"My love, I must."

They retrieved their glasses of wine and ever so gently touched them to each other.

"Lemniscate."

"Lemniscate. Eternity."

They then drank.

Part Three
Chapter 27
20**05**

I'm hot

I'M HOT. I'M HOT. I'M HOT.
I can't breathe because I'm hot. Really?

They were talking about her sister. Literally behind my back in back of me.
"I don't know," he was telling her." "But we've got a million meatballs."
Beth laughed.
Roger laughed.
I laughed.

It's a silly thing, we've got some good meatballs here," he said.

My pills. I was skipping my pills. No, no logic, no timing nor any reason – yes, one logic and one reason that only I knew.
Days went by.
Things were just a little different, good but different but same but different– and only I knew it......or so I thought.

I'm cold. I'm cold. I'M COLD.
I thought.
He's sleeping.

I thought.

I need to move.

I quietly crossed the room and gently picked up my leather jacket, opened the front door and stepped out. Quietly.

I'm alone.

I thought.

I need to get some air. I walked to the elevator and waited for it to open. I stepped inside, pressed for the ground floor and took a corner. The elevator opened, and I stepped into the lobby and outside to the street. I crossed in the middle of the street, looking both ways. The bright red lit lights from the furniture store glowed brightly – and around the corner. I walked. I thought. Roger, my love, my best friend Roger, friend – my oldest friend Amber – Amber lives in Jersey – Jersey, my friend Dena Maguire came from Jersey – Dena Maguire is pregnant – She must be in Methodist Hospital AND SHE NEEDS ME!!!!!! Oh, my GOD, SHE NEEDS ME!!!!!!!

I ran across the street to the bagel store that was open and very lit up.

"Please. Tell me a car service number."

They looked at me with a condescending look in their eye.

"HEY MAN! GIVE ME THE PHONE NUMBER!"

They no longer looked at me with a condescending look in their eye.

I dialed the number that they gave me.

I stepped outside.

I waited. The car came, and I got in and told him to take me to Methodist Hospital in Brooklyn and I sat back and relaxed in the car service and thought about my friend Dena Maguire. I sat in the car and thought about my friend Dena Maguire.

I got to Methodist.
I told them that I was there because Dena was having a baby!
I told them that I was there because Dena was having a baby!
I told them that I was there because Dena was having a baby!

They told me to lay down.

They told me To put my arms down.
They told me To put my arm out.
They told me To take it in.
They told me To shake it off.

My room had tea bags.
I had tea bags. Two of them that said "Twinnings." I thought
that was very clever.
I made Tea.
I skipped group meetings.
I HATED TO SHOWER
IT SCARED ME
There was a front door that led to the outside elevator. The
window in the door had lines in it, on a diagonal. This door shut
and kept me from leaving even if I wanted to. Leave.

Take this.
Take this pink pill, and this little pill, and this half pill, and this
round pill and this small round pill.
OKAY
And again
Take this pink pill, and this little pill, and this half pill, and this
round pill and this small round pill.

OKAY
And again
Take this pink pill, and this little pill, and this half pill, and this round pill and this small round pill.
OKAY

And again
Take this pink pill, and this little pill, and this half pill, and this round pill and this small round pill.

I had dreams of a dark man, of HIM, HE was agitated and upset with me, longing for me, needing me. The dreams dissipated as quickly as they came upon my wakening, but the feelings that the dreams brought on persisted. In my dreams HE paced and cursed–scaring me yet oddly comforting me at the same time.

And again
Taking this pink pill, and this little pill, and this half pill, and this round pill and this small round pill.

OKAY, OKAY, OKAY feeling better.
Really.
OKAY feeling better.

Where ever you go
Every seed you sow
Know that I'm with you

Chapter 28
2005

I took my pills

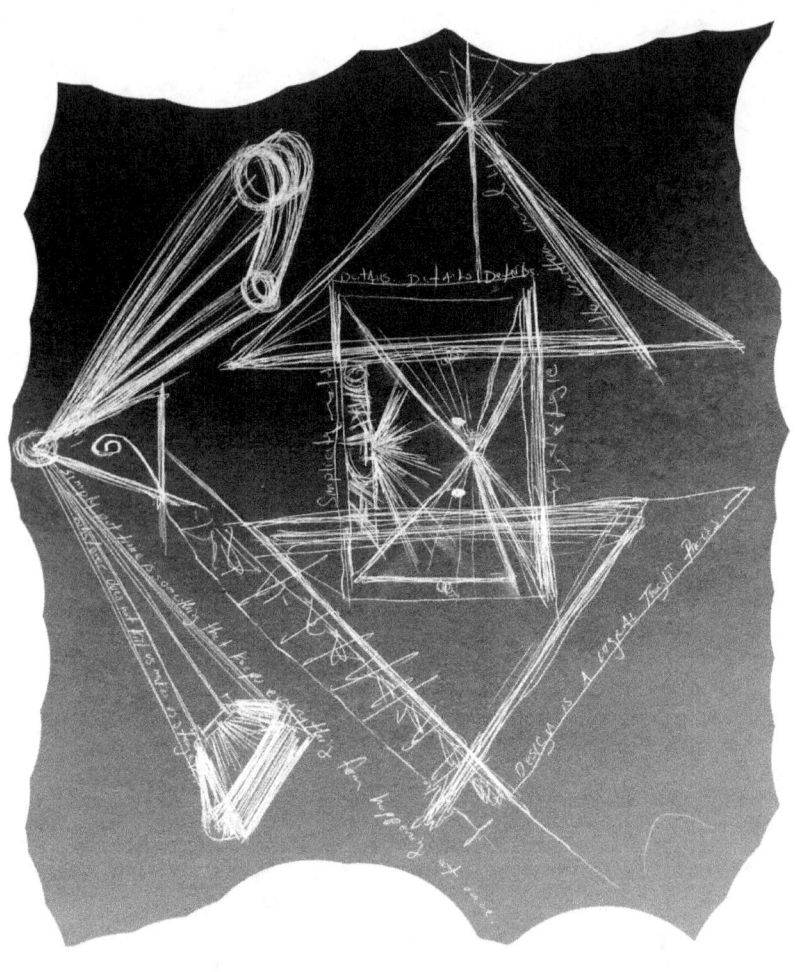

I got home. Roger had come to pick me up from the hospital again. We were married now. We had been for the past 5 years. Roger played out with Tony and Phil – and their band "Rachel Got Arrested"–more often than not. I hadn't smoked a cigarette in many many years and tried to keep up with dying my gray streak. Marybeth had moved to Australia of all places – the woman-child had a child of her own. My old boss Michael now owned a restaurant (properly branded of course) on the Jersey shore. He had gotten very tired of the publishing trade. My mother still drove me crazy, but also made me smile equally as much. My dear father was gone many years, as was my beloved cat Leo. I've had my graphic business, Wizage Media, with my best friend Olivia for the past 10 years in New Jersey. Olivia and I completed each other in ways that only she and I knew. I was her blue sky, calming her fears when the business was rough, and she was my rock, taking control with a steady hand. She was the most compassionate, intelligent, and talented woman I had ever met. Our respect was mutual, as was our love for each other. We had our ups and downs, our crazy days and had traveled the US together on numerous and ludicrous business trips. At the end of the day Wizage Media supported our lives.

"Welcome home baby," Roger said as we walked in the door of our apartment. "Let's hope you stay put."

I looked around our apartment, our home, at all of the things that made this place ours. I saw lots of my artwork and handicrafts, I saw lots of guitars, a piano, and a tambourine. I saw my Roger. He was much better, truer, and more responsible than he ever was before we were married. Huh. Imagine that. He was still mine, still cooked for me and still took care of me. Still played rock-n-roll.

"Cass, we have to talk."

"Yes, I would think so."

"Why is this happening? Why are you winding up in the hospital? What is the matter? Sometimes I feel like I should be the one in the hospital. Am I missing something here?"

I sat down on the couch.

"I'll tell you the truth. These pills I take, that I've been taking for most of my life, they keep me well, but they keep me LEVEL, TOO LEVEL. I can't FEEL anything except being calm, unemotional. I LIKE to have highs and lows, I LIKE to feel PASSIONATE, to feel HUMAN AND ALIVE. I'd like to throw out my pills for once and for all or maybe just dull the pill effect with alcohol. WHAT makes one human? Feelings, emotions, wants and needs. I WANT TO FEEL MY EMOTIONS."

He looked at me. "Baby, I understand, really, but I'm just afraid that one day you just won't bounce back to me."

"So I will promise to keep to my meds. I promise."

I took my pills in the morning.
I took my pills in the evening.
I took my pills in the morning.

I took my pills in the evening.

Over and over. Day after day after month after year. And I did drink and dull the effect of the pills with the beer and the wine, which seemed to work out just ducky.

That Feeling

But one day— it didn't matter that I was still taking the meds, it was that things were just a little different, good but different but same but different– it came and went –and only I knew it...

Chapter 29
2010

Wipe away a tear

So.
My Bride.
My lover.
Love of my life.
The "IN" to my "sane".
She's IN.
She's OUT.
She's OUT OF HER MIND.
–but burrowed deep in my soul.

Roger picked up his cell phone to call any one of a multitude of friends, just to set his mind at ease that someone loved him, and then slammed down the phone just as quickly.

He picked up the acoustic guitar from its spot in the corner of the room and began strumming.

I put on my happy face for you
Wipe away a tear for you
Don't care what they say 'bout you
Their money's green
But they don't make sense.

He looked at the guitar and gently returned it to it's corner, it was not the fix that he needed.

He crossed the room to the kitchen hitting the light switch on the wall. The bulb in the kitchen light blew out leaving him in the dark. His energy was strong tonight. The ambient light from the street was enough to see with. He reached into the closet for the pot pipe already full with weed, waiting. Looking for a lighter in the junk drawer he found a book of matches that would suffice. He pulled off 2 matches and lit the pipe. Drawing the smoke into his lungs – deeply – working the carburetor hole, then more deeply and then giving in to a hearty cough or two or three.
He waited.
He was still restless.
He changed the channel, made the TV louder and sunk into the sweet spot on the couch.
He focused his blue eyed gaze to the fish, Fred, on the shelf on the bookcase.
"Poor Fred, can't ever hide, can you?"
He stood up facing the open windows, facing the beautiful bridge that she loved so much.
My bride.
My lover.
Love of my life that draws OUT my insane.
He picked up the delicate wine glass sitting on the table. Caressing the fragile stem between his hands.
A bolt of anger tickled his being. He looked around wanting to find a wall to throw the innocent glass at – when he heard her key in the door.
She's home.

He put down the wine glass and greeted her at the door with a sardonic smile on his face.

I kissed him hello and walked past him into the apartment, one look at his eyes told me something was very wrong. I looked around but nothing seemed out of place.

"Hey, you Okay? You look like you've seen a nasty ghost."
"All good," he said.
"Okay, then..."
He got comfortable on the couch to watch reruns. I put my bag down in the hall and went inside to change.

"Fly a kite
On afternoons
In rainbow fields
Or in sand dunes"

"What?" I called from the other room. I could barely hear him speaking, almost chanting.

"Who am I to push my luck
Hitchhike to Miami
A pick up truck
To close the space from the girl who knew me"

I walked back into the living room to find him in the same spot, staring at the TV and speaking...
He looked at me and said:

"Back and forth
Hitchhike all night
Till I see you
Draped in blue
But it's just a dream"

I sat down next to him.
He smiled at me.
"Sometimes a quiet man is not a strong man."

He jumped up clapping his hands twice and rubbing them together.

"My love–
look at you–
so beautiful–
shall we dance?"

He extended his left hand to me and pulled me roughly by my arm off of the couch and into his embrace.
   We danced to a silent orchestra, twirling, dipping and swaying... for a moment, for a day.

The wind was whipping about outside and the sound that it made beat upon the windows like softened drums.

And we danced.

"Blinded by your beauty, my love," he whispered in my ear.
"Hurting from your grace." He shouted at me, holding me afar

from himself with outstretched arms – eyes ablaze with torment as I winced from the dichotomy between the cruelty of his tone and his actual words.

Pushing me aside he went to the piano on the other side of the room and sat down on the old bench that shook from the impact. Hands poised above the keys he held the pose for a moment and then dove into playing a melody, a song, his song, the soundtrack to the anguish that settled at these times within his soul. Hard and loud, repetitive and syncopated. He beat at the keys with purpose and intent. Music flew from his fingertips, notes ricocheted off the walls as the middle C remained silent from past abuse. Suddenly the tune became soft and hauntingly sweet as he played only on the right side of the piano... slowly, he ended with a flutter of the last three white keys. He looked up at me, a smile played tag upon his lips.

"It takes such courage to be able to create."

Tears suddenly fell from his eyes. His beautiful denim blue eyes now red. So sad. So incredibly sad. The extent and depth of his sadness always took me by surprise.... when the beast was awoken.

I approached him, holding his head to my breast softly.

"I'm here." I said to him.

I reached around him and held tightly like times before.

"I hear your words and your sorrow, I worry for your thoughts and where they take you. I'm always here."

We stood like that for a long time until he finally calmed down.

Chapter 30
2010

Mashed potatoes

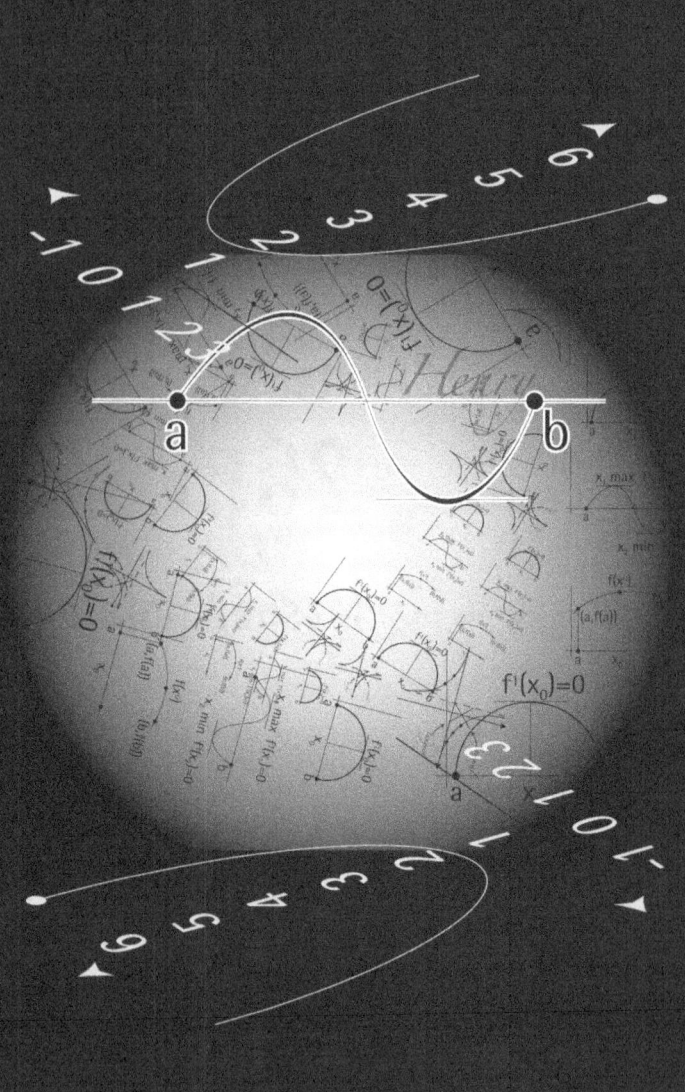

I moved deeper into the couch, deeper into the pillow, deeper into my dream.

My father stood before me looking tall, young, thin, with a full head of brown hair. He wore a dark blazer–a gold emblem of a crescent moon on his breast pocket.

Sta-Static-Black and White Static

He stood in the front of a college classroom. The stadium seating was filled with students. I sat near the back and near the center. The blackboard behind him was blank.

He spoke:

"Black holes are very likely the most unique anomalies in the universe."

Behind him a chalk drawing of a spheroid appeared onto the blackboard. He reached out his hand to pick up a long pointer from thin air and aimed it to the image.

"Gravity collected from the mass is so colossal that nothing can escape."

Sta-Static-Black and White Static

The lights flickered in the classroom and when I looked around half of the students were gone. The blackboard was blank.

He spoke:

"Seven new earth-like planets have been found in a relatively nearby solar system."

Behind him a chalk drawing of the planets drafted onto the blackboard. He took the pointer in his hand and named the individual exoplanets that were less than 40 light-years away.

Sta-Static-Black and White Static

The lights flickered in the classroom and I found myself the only one sitting there.

He looked up at me. The blackboard was blank.

"Hello pussycat." His pointer in hand.

The black board drew in the following schematic:

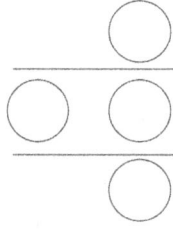

He pointed to the bottom circle.

"Earth."

He pointed to the left circle.

"Dark Matter / Parallel Universes. He pointed to the mid circle.

"The –"

Sta-Static-Black and White Static

He pointed to the top circle.

"Heaven."

"Believe, my dear, just believe.

Heaven is real."

Sta-Static-Black and White Static
Mountains.
I was alone on a mountain.

"Cassidy, wake up, I want you to hear this."

I turned over on the couch, tearing my dream away and watching it fade.
"I have something, a beginning of a song for me, Tony, and Phil." Roger said.
He was sitting next to me on the couch. He had in his hands his acoustic guitar.
"Listen. This is for you. I'm sorry about last night."

He watched his hands. He sang.

How long
Would you
Remember everything

"Wait, wait."
He shook his head and started again.
He stared at his fingers strumming the Yamaha.

How long
Would you
Remember everything I forgot to do
I'm in the mountains

"Wait, wait, one more time—"

He took a deep breath, tapped his foot, and looked at me.

How long
Would you
Remember everything
I forgot to do
I'm in the mountains
Trying to see
What I might find
Wake up little girl
And be mine
Be mine
Mashed potatoes
Don't mean gravy
So wake up little girl
And be mine

He smiled at me and I smiled at him.

Chapter 31
2010

The Vagabonds Kiss

"Roger, I'm leaving Friday, you know."

"Yes, I know, I know your flight's at 2:00, we need to leave for Jersey at 11:00, not like you've told me no less than a thousand times."

"Thanks, darling, I'm so excited, New Orleans with Olivia, my bass playing, partner, queen."

"No worries, I get it, I'll drive you on time."

Finally, a vacation with Olivia that had nothing to do with work. We both loved New Orleans, especially the secret restaurant with the amazing burgers across the street from the convention center and the fantastic stores in the French Quarter.

Roger drove me to Olivia's house on Friday, transporting my new luggage to Marc's car. He left soon after towards home.

Marc, Olivia's husband, drove us to Newark Airport, dropping us off with a big kiss to Olivia and a little kiss to me.

Our trip was from Friday to Monday, just enough to relax and have a good time.

Olivia and I found our way to the self check in, checked our bags because why deal with our baggage?

We made our way through security and on to get something to eat.

We ate breakfast with our faces in our phones and then made our way to the departure gate.

The call for boarding started not long after and we entered the plane.

All good.

After many trips to many places we had agreed long ago that the best solution was to each sit on the aisle.

The plane filled.

The pilot welcomed everyone, and the stewardess showed us how to behave.

The plane took off and as tradition held it, Olivia and I looked at each other, smiling as the plane ascended.

I took out my book and leaned back to read and relax. Olivia took out her earphones to listen to her music.

Two and a half hours later the pilot announced that we were about to land.

We adjusted our seats to be upright, we closed our trays and readied ourselves for the landing.

In past times passengers would clap upon landing, but not in these days.

We left the plane and searched for the ladies' room, then searched for our luggage, then searched for a cab.

Our hotel, The Vex Hotel on Canal Street, welcomed us with flowing white curtains from floor to a very high ceiling, a beautiful red lighted bar, a fancy restaurant set with candelabras and gold place settings that no one seemed to enter. We took our luggage in hand and rode up the elevator to the sixth floor. The elevator doors opened to reveal dark hallways lit only with dim lights. We found our room and laughed to each other that this was not the "typical" room we were used to.

As Olivia and I unpacked, I realized that I had made a colossal mistake by not packing my pills. Oh! I didn't tell Olivia as I didn't want to worry her, but I told myself that this was not going to ruin our trip.

At about 5:30 after unpacking, we changed into lighter clothes, comfortable shoes for walking and set out for the French Quarter. The Quarter was packed with many, many tourists, young and old. We made our way first to Bourbon Street for posterity. Beads were strewn about left over from Fat Tuesday. It seemed like everyone was young and drunk, holding plastic glasses filled with hurricane drinks. The streets themselves smelled overwhelmingly like vomit. Taking a selfie in front of the Bourbon Street sign and then deleting it on both our phones because we didn't like the way we looked, we vowed not to post any photos of ourselves. Our mission was to find the restaurant that we loved on a SW corner, next to a NW corner or something like that. We wandered the streets and amazingly finally found the restaurant.

Small round tables were scattered about the front entranceway. We went to the back of the restaurant decorated predominantly with black and white tiles and a large bar. Oysters! We both loved oysters with crackers and hot sauce and lemon. We ordered four orders of oysters stemming from around the eastern US. Salad, fresh fish of the day, a dirty martini with four olives for Olivia and a light beer for me. We were stuffed by the end of the meal. Stuffed and the night had passed.

"Full?" she asked.

"Walk home and then sleep?" she said to me.

"Absolutely." I replied.

Traveling and eating was very tiring.

We made our way back to the Hotel.

Canal Street was filled with homeless people. We had not seen so many indigent souls since our time in NY many years ago. It was quite unnerving, as was the dimly lit hallways of our hotel.

SATURDAY

Olivia awoke early as usual. I could have slept till noon.

"C'mon, let's go explore," she said.

We took a bus to the west side of New Orleans.

We scoured the stores.

We loved the municipal graphic designs prevalent in this part of town.

We ate black-eyed gumbo.

I bought earrings.

We loved the store selling hand-made metal letters and words and bought goodies for the office.

We took selfies that were just for us.

I felt great.

"You know where we're going tonight?" I said.

"Oh yes, I know." She smiled.

Mikkel's was our favorite.

We dressed and took off for Jackson Square.

"Do you have a reservation?" the young girl asked us.

Olivia smiled to me and said, "Of course."

"Olivia."

The girl looked and looked and said, "I'm sorry but I don't see your reservation."

"Just take one more look," Olivia said with a wink to me.

And she did, and said, "I'm sorry, I've got it right here. Let me show you to your table."

The table was covered with a white cloth.

The walls were covered with purple velvet flocked wall paper and gilded framed portraits of people long gone. The bar was lit with amber lights and top shelf liquor. Raw brick surrounded the back wall and the walls facing the courtyard.

The restaurant was packed with good looking people, laughing, eating, and drinking. We took our seats, and put our pristine white napkins on our laps like good girls.

An adorable young waiter in a black tuxedo approached us.

"Dirty martini with four olives but not too dirty," Olivia said.

"Vagabonds Kiss," I said.

"That's Ketel One Citron, balsamic-cranberry gastrique, and lemon juice," the young beautiful waiter-man said.

"Yes, please."

Olivia gave me a look that said that's not your usual.

"Whatever," I said.

We consulted the menu.

"You order," I said.

The waiter came back, looking even better than before, if that was possible. He was tall with long dark hair and striking blue eyes. His black tuxedo fit him like a glove and the black bow tie framed his chiseled jaw.

"What will it be ladies?"

Olivia held the menu up and read—

"Jumbo lump crab cake to share for our appetizer.

Roasted beet salad to share.

And we'll both have pan crusted salmon for our entree."
Money was no object when we traveled.
We drank our cocktails, reveling in the atmosphere that was so familiar.
"Can't wait to go to the Mikkel's reading lounge," Olivia said.
"Me too."
We enjoyed our meal, our two rounds of drinks, no dessert for us nor coffee.
We ordered two more drinks and took them with us at the end of our meal.

The reading lounge
We went upstairs and around and upstairs to the empty reading lounge.
The room was lit with red bulbs.
It was adorned in red brick, red, there were red heavy curtains hanging, red.
There were frightening ceramic masks adhered to the walls.
Couches of red velvet and warm red colors lined the room.
An ancient table was dead center in the lounge.
Tall statues stood in the two far corners.
Large tufted chairs welcomed us.
Framed images of sexy ladies from the 1920s hung on the walls.
Tall lamps with soft light enveloped the space.
The lights were low.
The music was soft.
I felt like I was home.
"I love this room," I said.
"I LOVE THIS ROOM," I said.
"I know, take it easy," Olivia said.

"NO, YOU DON'T UNDERSTAND, I LOVE THIS ROOM."

"Cass, easy, girl, stop yelling, you're going to make a scene."

"YELLING, WHO'S YELLING?"

"YOU ARE," she screamed.

"It's the Vagabonds Kisses," Olivia said.

"Yes, the Vagabonds Kisses, you're right."

Five women walked into the lounge.

One tall and thin and dressed in a small black dress.

One short and fat and dressed in a long flowered pantsuit.

One very pretty with straight blonde hair.

One very short with very curly dark hair.

One very ugly with a fabulous figure and holding a large red candle.

"Hello ladies, heard you were in here, please, join us for the séance," said the very ugly woman.

Olivia and I looked at each other.

"Of course, I'm Olivia and this is my friend Cassidy, thank you ever so much for the invitation."

"I'm Aurora, and these are my four friends, Blake, Elizabeth but we call her Lisa, Emma and AnnMarie."

We all gave a smile to each other.

"Come." Aurora said as she shut the door that had led into the lounge.

"I am actually THE Mikkel's great granddaughter born and bred in this beautiful city, and I have every right to be here and conduct these séances so no worries. My ancestors have indulged in these séances for many generations. Hence the name of the 'Mikkel's Reading Lounge'." She walked over to one of the statues in the corner tilting back its head and changed the music.

"I hope you enjoy Macbeth, a European heavy metal band from Stockholm, heavy metal, yes, but melodic and diverse, incorporating progressive, folk, blues, classical, and jazz influences into their heavy metal music."

Aurora then walked over to the other statue in the corner, tilting back its head, and took out seven sticks of incense.

"I have here seven sticks of incense representing each one of us. Blake, please distribute."

Blake took the incense and placed them around the room into holders that we hadn't noticed before and lit them with a red lighter that she took from her bra.

Olivia and I were stunned to be here at this time and surprised to be included in whatever was to happen.

"Chairs, ladies," Aurora said.

Blake, Lisa, Emma and AnnMarie moved the large tufted chairs, seven of them, to the middle of the room surrounding the ancient table.

"Sit," said Aurora. And we did.

"We are here to conduct a séance, an attempt to communicate with the spirits that have passed. Our emphasis is placed on spiritual values. We mean no harm, we are gathered in gratitude and love."

"We are gathered in gratitude love," the four women replied

"We will attempt to answer questions or deliver messages. Our only question is that all present shall believe it is possible to communicate with the other side."

"Yes, I do," said Blake.

"Yes I do," said Elizabeth.

"Yes I do," said Emma.

"Yes I do," said AnnMarie.

"Yes, I do," Olivia said. I knew she didn't.

"Yes, I do," I replied and I certainly did.

Aurora continued.

"Most people tend to fear what cannot be fully understood and, therefore, if we experience a successful séance, we will undoubtedly be left with a sense of wonder and appreciation for the otherworld that is beyond what we can see or touch. We will now close our eyes and take a moment of silence for all of us to think of the deceased person that we would like to contact and a yes or no question that we might like to ask them."

After a moment she took the large red candle and placed it in the center of the table.

"Lighter, Elizabeth."

Elizabeth reached into her bra and took out the red lighter and handed it to Aurora.

Aurora took the lighter and lit the candle.

"All present, please take hands and keep hands whatever may be."

The women took each other's hands.

The music played softly in the background.

"Lisa, may we ask cordially for your husband to join us. His passing has been recent, and we ask kindly for him to show us his presence."

Lisa closed her eyes tightly.

"Tony, are you okay?" Lisa said.

We all sat silently, and a drum was heard above the music.

"He was a drummer," Lisa said.

The drum percussion continued as the women listened and then faded out.

"Blake, your sister has passed in the last year and we ask kindly for her to show us her presence."

Blake closed her eyes tightly.

"Sophia, are you happy? Blake said.

We all sat silently and an unexpected wind blew through the room.

A wind chime sounded, and all held their hands tightly.

"She loved wind chimes," Blake said.

"Emma, may we kindly ask your mother to join us. Her passing has been sudden."

Emma closed her eyes tightly.

"Mama, have you met with Daddy?" Emma said.

We felt the table shake and the curtains shimmer.

"Yes, my Emma, I love you," we heard through the shimmer.

Emma started to cry softly.

"AnnMarie, your brother is gone for some time now, we ask kindly for him to show us his presence."

AnnMarie closed her eyes tightly.

"Michael, have you acclimated to where you are?"

The room got very warm and a scent of delicious food took over the space.

"He was a chef," AnnMarie said as they lifted their faces to take in the smell.

"My new friends, please tell me who you would like to contact," Aurora said.

Olivia looked at me.

I spoke.

"I, I, I,"

I closed my eyes tightly.

At once the curtains began to billow, one by one by one.

The masks fell off of the walls and flew across the room and banged off the opposite walls.

Music – it began to get louder and louder and LOUDER.
The loud music bass shook the room.

Wherever you go
Every seed you sow
Know that I'm with You

The framed paintings found themselves twisting and turning
in a dance to the music.
The table rose into the air turned and the candle on the table
grew to astronomical size rising to the ceiling still lighted.
The chairs that we were sitting on took flight into the air, and
we all fell to the floor screaming.
The lights were blinking on and off and on and off and on and
off.
The mirror above the red couch cracked into fragments slowly
and then broke into a million tiny pieces.

There was a voice enormous and astounding.
YOU HAVE SUMMONED ME
THE RULES MUST BE BROKEN.
THE RULES MUST BE BROKEN.
BROKEN, THE RULES MUST BE BROKEN.

THE ROOM WAS VIBRATING AND PULSATING AND SHAK-
ING –
THE RED LIGHTS WERE BLINKING
AURORA WAS SCREAMING AS WERE THE OTHER LADIES
WITH THEIR HANDS COVERING THEIR EARS.

Olivia sat on the floor in peace and comfort, watching the antics before her –

"enough enough ENOUGH!" she said.

And it stopped.

The next thing I knew I woke up in the hotel.

"If you must ask me –YES, that was some Vagabonds Kiss? huh?" I said.

"I didn't ask you."

"Oh."

SUNDAY

We woke up the next morning. Olivia slept longer than she usually did, and I had slept soundly.

We never mentioned the night before.

Seafood House

Lunch

We found a cute restaurant and ate at a picnic table.

After we searched for gifts for our employee family. Frank got a Devil's bobblehead.

We stopped into House of Voodoo and bought lots of things and I brought home magnets for the fridge.

Dinner was mellow. We went to the restaurant across from the convention center where we had the very best burgers imagined.

Where ever you go
Every seed you sow
Know that I'm with you

MONDAY
Airport at 11:30
A nice breakfast at noon.

Chapter 32
2015

Know that I'm with you

143

We laid in bed, sleeping late. 11:00

"Cass, you up?" he said.

"I'm up."

"Cass, I had a bad dream."

"What honey?"

"I dreamed that I died."

"It was just a dream."

"I went to heaven, my Aunt Paula was there, and my father was there, and there was a big party going on."

He gave a heavy sigh.

"Do you believe in heaven?" he said.

I took a few moments to answer.

"Roger, I believe that we go where we belong and if heaven is the place then I do believe in heaven."

He put his arms around me and held me tightly.

"Cass, come, let's go."

I grabbed my jacket from the hall closet and walked out of the apartment to the elevator with him.

We walked down the street, around the corner and stopped in front of the garage door that embraced the facade of the bar.

Standing and mingling with friends in front of the bar, I noticed a truck parked. A young man at the helm turned to give me a smile. I turned to Rog and quickly turned back around to the driver, but he was gone. Or had never been there? I got a poke feeling in my upper stomach. HA. I told Roger that I was going to the ladies' room and walked into the bar. Familiar patrons populated the establishment. I walked toward the back and saw out of the corner of my eye a group of women, older women. At closer range there were a group of about 20 in age from maybe 50-85. All of them were wearing purple clothing and a fancy red hats. One hat had tall red feathers, one was a beret, another had a flower and rhinestone detail, they were all different. Ahhhhhhhhhhhhhh! Was this the mother of all hallucinations? One of the women passed by me walking toward the bathroom and TOUCHED MY ARM!!!!! AHHHHHHHHHHH! I stepped closer to the group and one of them noticed me looking.

"Hello dear," she said.

"Hi there." I didn't quite know what to say.

"This is the Crimson Group."

"Really, the Crimson Group."

"Yes, we are a group of women over 50 that meets once a month to celebrate friendship and embrace our lives and where we are within them. We eat, drink, have fun and get dressed up in our purple clothes and our beautiful red hats." She smiled broadly at me. I was so taken aback by this that I started to laugh. Oh boy, if I was imagining this, well then I was really sick. Tony, the owner of the bar, came up to me and smiled.

"Pretty cool, huh?" he said.

I woke up and walked into the kitchen. it was an overcast day–the light was obscured by the curtains. I took my pills. Fred the fish on the mantle needed to be fed. As I opened the curtain, the gray blue of the day washed the living room with sweet gray color.

The iced tea's cover in the fridge showed me a lovely word definition.

Lemniscate is the sign for eternity.

I went to the computer.

In algebraic geometry, a lemniscate may refer to any of several figure-eight or –∞– shaped curves.

A lemniscate is a plane curve with a characteristic shape, consisting of two loops that meet at a central point. The curve can also be known as the lemniscate of Bernoulli among others. The lemniscate, reduced in size to that of typographical characters, is commonly used as the symbol for infinity, or for a value that increases without limit. Also:

The Devil's curve, a curve defined by the quartic equation $y^2 (y^2 - a^2) = x^2 (x^2 - b^2)$ in which one connected component has a figure-eight shape.

I was so excited to have found this marvelous term that I had never known for something that brought me closer to my father the perpetual science student.

Hmmmm, interesting, delicious, marvelous and wonderful. Eternity – ha, Devil's curve. LOVE this.

Ahhhhhhhhhhh! All of a sudden I felt HIM. I held onto the kitchen counter looking into the window. ----------------I FELT HIM.

Come love, it's been such a very , very, very, very, very, llllllllll-loooooooooooonnnnnnngggggg time. HE said. Where have you run to? What have you been and where have you seen?"

How is our countryside, I miss it so, the butterfly beats his wings quickly and surely and the time passes.

I insist, I still feel you in my heart but once again and once more I must say to you that the time is not here. I am still here, and I want to be here. I don't know how else to tell you, you have followed me this whole life. We have made a deal, we have rules for this deal, what more can I say and what more can I do. You long for me and at times I long for you too, but the time IS NOT NOW – so farewell for now my love.

"Cass come, let's go," Roger said.

I grabbed my jacket from the hall closet and walked out of the apartment to the elevator with him.

Sunglasses on, we walked toward the bridge. The April sun felt good on my black leather shoulders although it was weak because of the hour. We did not speak, just walked at an even pace.

That feeling

Things were just a little different, good but different but same but different – and only I knew it......

The flowering trees were as pretty above as they were below on the sidewalk where they had blown and scattered. One tree hung dangerously low, more beautiful than the next. Small families were playing together, and the basketball court was filled.

Ahhhhh, feeling good. Looking up the underbelly of the Verrazzano bridge, I could feel the geometric dark sandy concrete pieces suspended gently above as if by feathers or strings. Ha! Quite beautiful. The beautiful Fort Hamilton – Major Nelson and Jeannie lived there. We walked through "Cannonball Park" across the Belt Parkway exit and over to the deck promenade facing the Atlantic Ocean under the bridge. The water was blue, so dark that it was just almost black. We gazed out across the lazy Saturday morning at boats that were sailing and crossing beneath the bridge.

"I'll make you a deal," I said.

I said, I said, I said. Make a deal with me, my dark darling.

"Okay," Roger said.

"I'll feed Fred for a week if you make love to me tonight."

A smile came across his face, his blue eyes sparkled.

"Deal."

Later we drove to Nostrand Avenue. We crossed the busy street to the Jupiter Grocery where raw clams were found, our favorite. We bought two bunches, a dozen to each bunch and headed home with the groceries and the clams in the trunk on cushions of ice.

We looked for a spot, a challenge, listening to classic rock, his preference.

We unpacked the groceries and Roger began his cooking magic in our small efficient kitchen. Roger's cooking skills were second to none, and he gladly cooked every gourmet meal that we ate. Garlic, my job, he opened the cloves with a push of his hand on a large knife. I cut the top and bottom off of each clove then peeled the angelic skin. He took the garlic and held a cutting knife from the front angle, bringing the back angle up and down slicing in rhythm, in logic, in timing. The breadcrumbs, he spiced it with fresh lemon, olive oil, pepper, and basil and sage and flavored it with love and passion, prepping it for the coating. The clams, he took a thin knife and held the clam in his left hand while shucking them open with his right discarding the top shell. The pan, he took an aluminum cooking pan and poured in white cooking wine, a bit of water and parsley.

Placing the clams decorated with the mixture into the pan, he rubbed his hands together and said "Are you ready?"

"No." I laughed.

He laughed. "Me neither. "

He walked across the room to fetch a bottle of Pinot Noir. He brought it back to the kitchen and reached down to get the bottle opener. Pouring the wine into two glasses, he spoke to me.

"You made me a deal today, now go feed our fish."

I walked across the room, took out the beta pellets and fed Fred.

As I returned to the kitchen, he held out a glass of wine to me in a toast.

"Here's to Fred, long may he live."

We clinked our glasses.

We drank our wine.

We drank the bottle of Pinot Noir, laughing and having fun and then half of the bottle of Burgandy.

He walked into the living room where I was standing.

"Take off your shirt."

And I did.

"Take off your pants."

And I did.

"Mute the TV."

And I did as he took off his shirt and his pants and we stood there in only our underwear.

"Come."

He stood above me spreading my arms open wide as he looked into my eyes, his radiating with love and hunger.

The television flashed lights as if lightening had entered the room. A face, RED, a face, HIS face. HE had entered the room, I could sense HIM practically smell HIM.

"OH!" I cried out at Roger's touch.

OH! – You come to me at my most intimate moments. THIS IS NOT FAIR. Respectfully I say I know what it is that you want, but you know what my wishes are and we both know our rules – I STILL LIVE AS A HUMAN.

Where ever you go
Every seed you sow
Know that I'm with you

HIS essence moved out of the room.

Roger moved his hands over my body and then he moved into me, into me, oh, good God. Into me...

I got up and put on the radio
Where ever you go
"Ready to eat?"

Chapter 33
2015

The holy jester

Mid July, a hot summer Saturday. BBQ at Helene and Ricky's as was the norm. Helene was Roger's first girlfriend, if that was the right term for a six-year-old who had protected him from bullies on the way home from school way back when. He loved her dearly to this day as he loved her husband, and I too loved all his dear old friends. We drove to Staten Island with Beth and Doug in the back seat, anticipating the day to come which was always a guaranteed good time. Suddenly Roger lowered the radio.

"Cassidy, tell us, how is the traffic and weather out there today."

I laughed aloud.

"It's a scorcher today, 89 degrees real feel temperature of 95. Traffic is moving well on the west bound Staten Island Expressway. I see no accidents up ahead. Back to you in the studio, Rog."

Roger and I laughed at each other and Beth and Doug looked at each other. We stopped at the local gas station for beer. We had made it there in no time, although a bit late for the call time. We parked in the cull de sac, making sure that we were lined up to let others park as well. We walked in the front door where their lab mix dog Coco greeted us with barks. Everyone was a little scared of Coco as she had an enormous presence and spirit.

"Hello, we're here," Roger called.

Helene greeted us at the door.

"Well, it's about time." She laughed.

The deck was full of friends and drinks and food, as was the back yard. Tables with sun umbrellas, chairs and decorations. The flavor changed as we walked in because Roger was there. The party had begun. Roger was the life of the party, always, the one who made everyone laugh, sing, cry. The pool leading down from the deck beckoned for company and the sun was shining brightly, asking for someone to jump in. Ricky went into the house and made the music louder. 80s disco made everyone laugh and reminisce. Of course, Roger was the one to jump into the pool with his clothes on, calling out for someone to join him. Beth took the invite and put on her bathing suit and joined him in the pool. Helene threw a tootsie roll candy at Roger and he declared it "Doody."

"There's doody in the pool," he cried and everyone laughed.

Andy cried, "Alert, Doody in the pool."

"Hey Rog, how 'bout another doody?" Butchie called, holding up another tootsie roll.

"Yea, Rog, make it a double doody," Billy called.

The signature drink, bone crusher was flowing and everyone was having a good time.

Roger emerged from the pool, drying off and making his way through the crowd. You could follow his path with the laughs that he left behind. And then he danced, he spun, he fell, everyone clapped and applauded with glee and nothing made him happier, and nothing made me happier than to see him entertaining his crowd.

My man, the holy jester.

That was my Roger, the beautiful merrymaker. The man that made everyone smile and happy and always made us feel like our lives were the best, even if his was the worst.

Laura, Annette, Ricky, Helene, Butchie, Karen and I sat at a round table in the yard, feverishly discussing the merits of Italian food and baked clams. Baked clams always reminded me of love with Roger. He described his recipe to the group and asked for suggestions on his take of his dish. Laura added a spice to the mix, Karen suggested an addition to the pan sauce as well as a side dish and I just smiled, taking a movie of the roundtable discussion between the dear friends because I only do garlic, not create food to the level that Roger does.

I drank some more beer and I drank some wine and I drank some bone crushers. And I had to lay down. I left the crowd and made my way into the house, avoiding Coco, and went to the lounger upstairs to relax.

Comfortable in the living room, alone, I heard the music from outside. As I relaxed more I heard the music change to classical slowly, lowly, softly and lovingly as I drifted away.

"How are you my love? Are you having an earthly good time? No fear, I cannot see you, but I hear your heart beating. I know the way of your longings, but I still cannot understand the way of your yearning, to be of mortal and not with me. I am waiting, patiently and maddeningly, for your return. As of our deal, I bid you adieu. Sleep well, my lovely."

I stirred in my sleep and later slowly woke before anyone had discovered me.

I returned to the party, glad that I had slept off the drinks, because it was I that had to drive home. Roger was way past the point of operating a car.

One Saturday

We picked up Beth from the lobby.

"Ready?" Roger asked her."Yes," she said.

We walked to the parked car and took the ride down Ft. Hamilton Parkway to the Chinese grocery store. This was a treat. The store had vegetables unknown to anyone but the Chinese. They had fish, turtles, clams, crabs, pork, beef, lobsters, shrimp, shellfish, sushi and on and on. There were fish tanks with eels and trout and octopus. Pity on the turtles that were so alive waiting for death to become them.

Roger liked the scallions and the dumpling wrappers and the ginger and the fish sauce and the bean sauce. I liked the beautiful small dishes and the Chinese spoons. Beth liked whatever Roger liked because she was the one who concocted the dumplings like a machine out of the mixture that Roger made. We bought a dragon fruit just for the fun of it, even though none of us liked it.

While walking down the aisles, a pretty Chinese girl smiled at Roger.

"Ni hao? Nee hao mah?" Roger said.

"Wo hen hao!," she said, blushing and walking away.

"What was that all about?" Beth said.

I laughed. I had seen Roger do this before.

I turned to Beth.

"He said, "Hi how are you, the extent to which he knows Chinese. She probably said 'fuck you' or on the contrary 'doing good' from her reaction."

"Ha!" Roger laughed.

We paid and wrapped up our purchases and headed home, waiting for Andy, Beth's husband to join us.

August
Monday
I had taken a week off of work and instead of going to an island or a trip to the Poconos, Roger and I decided to paint the kitchen. In theory it sounded very easy but in practice it was quite the ordeal. We spent untold hours in Home Depot deciding on the colors, a rich chocolate, cherry brown, and a grassy, leafy green. Traditional glossy white for the ceiling. After choosing the colors, we were exhausted and decided to begin fresh the next day.

Tuesday
Having coffee and admiring the view of the Verrazzano bridge we began, we stripped down into our underwear and took two beers out of the fridge. We laid out the drop cloths and put the stereo on high, playing all our old favorite songs from our past. We settled on a repeat of "Miss Lady" for some odd reason.

Roger took control and I listened.

"Bring the ladder closer, get the smaller brush, don't drip the roller."

"We'll finish tomorrow," he said.

We ordered pizza as the kitchen was off limits to dry.

Wednesday
He took the knobs off the cabinets. We reached high for the ceiling and took our time getting the corners just right. We were quite proud of the job that we had done. He beckoned to me.

He took his finger and gently dipped it into the white paint and dabbed it onto my nose.

"Oh," I said with a smile.

"Lay down," he said with a bigger smile.

I laid down on the drop cloth.

He laid down on top of me leaning on his elbows.

"You're a very good girl. Good painter and good assistant."

He kissed me, careful of the white paint on my nose.

"I'm very proud of you." He smiled at me, his blue eyes sparkling.

I smiled back at him.

He held my arms as he took my tee shirt hem into his teeth, bringing it upward.

My stomach filled with butterflies.

He looked into my eyes.

"Look into my eyes. Who do you see?"

I looked for a moment in the reflection of his eyes.

"Me!"

"I love you so."

Chapter 34

2015

Thought you were a dancer

He called to me from the bedroom.

"Cass, vest or no vest?"

"Vest."

"Yeah, you think so?"

"Yes."

"Tie or no tie?"

"No tie."

"OK, I think so too."

"You sure about the white shirt?"

"Yes, very sure."

"Boots or sneakers?"

"Boots."

I was in the kitchen waiting for him to get ready for his show tonight.

"Come here and put this in."

I joined him in the bedroom where he stood fussing with his diamond stud earring, trying to put it in to the hole that was practically closed. The buzzer rang.

"That's Tony, get it," Roger said.

I let Tony into the lobby with the button on the wall.

Roger emerged with a pose for me.

"How do I look?"

His blue eyes twinkled, and his smile lit up the room.

"Honey, you look like a rock star," I said and reached up to kiss him.

The doorbell rang and there was Tony looking so handsome in his new black t-shirt, his case holding his bass in hand.

"Come in, come in."

Tony kissed me and hugged me dearly.

"Phil will be here any minute," Tony said.

The buzzer rang again.

"There you go–"

I pushed the button on the wall again, letting him into the lobby.

Phil rang the doorbell, looking tall and handsome in his own new black t-shirt.

"Come in, come in."

Phil kissed me and hugged me dearly.

Roger reached into the fridge and took out four beers.

"Cheers!" he said in a toast. "To Rachel Got Arrested!"

We all laughed, drank on the toast and finished our beers while the guys discussed the arrangements of the music for tonight. The boys would be playing in the local bar a block from our home. I grabbed the set lists that I had made – I was the fourth Beatle – and we were off.

The night was gentle, a soft wind blew on the April evening. We got to the bar and it was a flurry of setting up the drums, sound checks, making the mikes work correctly, and putting up the banner that I had created for them way back when with the band name, Rachel Got Arrested. The origin of the name came from a nondescript line of a movie that Roger had caught, and it had stayed with them for many years.

Friends filled the bar, so many friends.

Janine and Josh and Shari and Vinny and Michele and Brian and Carol and Marc and Mary and Eric and Lori and Donna and Doug and Laura and Butchie and Helene and Ricky and Faith and Mitch and Beth and Andy and Ro and Danny and Renee and Jenna and Mike and Billy and Karen and Lisa and John and Stacy and Tommy and Elise and Joe and Gayle and Jeff and Tracey and Pete and Stacey and Steve and Stacey and Phil and Bonnie and Todd and Larry and Marni and David and Milo and Janine and Christine and Justin and Frank and Nicole and Eric and Shara and Adam and Dave and Beney and Ross and Dana and Freddy and Alice and David and Michael and Amber and Johnny and Michelle and Tony and Annette and Louie and Annie and Adam and Rona and Baryne and Renee and Donna and Todd and Donna and Rich and Grace and Danny and Ro and Kevin and Margaret and Frank and Nicole and Gary and Wendy and Julie and Steven and Tracy and Esta and Howie and Kneller and Goody and Frank and Mike and Larry and Marni and Monique and Peter and John and Lisa and Ronnie and Nancy and Lauren and Joey and Angela and Tonyann and AnnMarie and Steve and and and and and and and and and... OH! there was such a crowd...

Tony the owner of the bar gave me a big smile.

I made my way through the crowd kissing, hugging and laughing with our friends.

The lights lowered.
The crowd settled in.
The band was introduced.

I was standing off to the side, stage left.

They started with "Thought You Were A Dancer," my personal favorite.

Roger stood in the spotlight, his electric guitar hanging off his shoulder and shooting off sparks of light. He took the mike in both hands, gave a broad smile to the crowd, and started singing.

Saw you standing waiting for a bus to east LA.
You been looking like

He held the note high and tight

You've been turned out in the rain
I can see your fate

Tony and Phil kicked in with bass and drums. Roger began playing his guitar.

Oh, so many people have come and gone
Nothing lasts too long
It's time I traveled onnnnn –
Oh yeah– Mama got it on in a red eyed zone
Couldn't get it on cause she was so alone

—Time is of the essence
A whisper in my ear
I spun around to look
But no one was there

THE CASSENDRE DECREE

Too much was never enough oh yeah
Thought you were a dancer
I thought you were a dancer

Driving into town
Top pulled down
Suns on your face
Such a big disgrace
You told me that you danced in a club downtown

_____

–Time is of the essence
Another whisper in my ear
I spun around to look
Still no one was there

_____

–I walked to the ladies' room– cowgirls
I was alone but could clearly hear the band:

And I stand here with nothing left
Time stood still.............

_____

Another whisper in my ear

_____

I HEAR YOU
She looked into the mirror
I HEAR YOU GOOD GOD I HEAR YOU

I HEAR YOU I HEAR YOU I HEAR YOU – I screamed
The mirror shattered from my scream
I turned around in a circle to see that the mirror was now intact
I HEAR YOU –
I screamed even louder
The mirror shattered once more
I turned around again, and the glass was there, intact
YOU
I stared into the mirror –
YOU can't understand that I AM TO BE HUMAN FOR AS LONG AS IT TAKES
The mirror shattered once again
I turned around slowly to see the pieces of the glass coming together and making their way to becoming intact
YOU MUST WAIT
WAIT I SAY
WAIT FOR ME
I AM NOT READY TO LEAVE THIS REALM
LEAVE ME BE I WILL BE WITH YOU SOON ENOUGH
The tiles of the ladies' room began to melt.
YOU MUST ADHERE TO OUR RULES
The toilet began to bubble and rumble loudly
She pulled her hair back away from her head
WHAT MUST I DO TO REMIND YOU TO TELL YOU TO ADVISE YOU THAT THIS IS NOT OVER– NOT YET
Suddenly HIS voice took over the space and faded to black as HE cried out –
"I WILL MAKE YOU HAPPYYYYYYYYYYYYyyyyyyy......'

My gray streak slowly took a firmer hold in the front of my head.

The music was playing:
Thought I'd get a job
I couldn't get a job
I picked it up and I married a snob
Too much was never enough

Too much is never enough
I left the ladies room feeling sick and nauseous. The guys were kicking ass. I took my place again, stage left and watched the rest of the concert, singing along to all of the songs.

Chapter 35

2015

The jam

Thursday

"Rog, it's time to go."

"Let's go," he said getting up from the couch.

He checked his guitar case, finished his beer, grabbed the Steele Blonde CD as well as his jacket, wallet, and lighter and we were off.

We crossed the Verrazzano Bridge, slid through the Staten Island Expressway and soared over the Goethels Bridge into New Jersey. A right on Stiles, a left on St. Georges, a left on Grand and voila we were there, with a little help from Steele Blonde.

The bar was crowded. This was jam night where anyone could get up and play with the house band filling in. The house band was now playing, Olivia was playing bass. Olivia was an incredibly talented musician, sexy as hell and took your breath away with her perfection of her understanding of music. It showed in every song she played, and male bass players showed her with homage at every turn. She looked at me and gave me a smile and looked at Roger and gave him a left wink. Marc, her husband, played drums and Steve, the magician, played guitar as did Big Mike. Alex on keyboard and Jimmy singing completed the band. The jam played classic rock, which was Roger's love. Roger looked around and scoped out the friends that he knew.

He leaned his guitar against the wall and waited his turn to play, a beer in hand.

The song ended, and they announced a break.

Olivia came over to me.

"Did you see Brien?"

"Yes, and I said hello."

"Did you see Ray?"

"Yes, and I said hello."

"What about George?"

"Yes, yes, yes."

"How do we sound?"

"Awesome."

"I'm going to get a drink and say hello to everyone."

"Okay, no problem."

"Later."

The band gathered together to start the second set of the jam.

"C'mon up Roger," Olivia said into the microphone.

Roger looked up and smiled. He took his guitar and stepped onto the stage floor.

His song was for drums, guitar and bass. He understood this configuration very well.

The song began.

Unbelievably, Roger had never yet played with Olivia and having been such family for so many years the intimacy was evident as they played and complemented each other.

Roger smiled as he played simply because he loved to play. It was his true passion.

He made love to his guitar as was his way of showing his affection for his Fender.

Olivia took her bass high into the sky, pointing it upward as was her trademark move.

Marc kept them together in his special way of mastering his drum set and his impeccable sense of timing.

And they played.

I took pictures. Little did we know it was the first and last time they would play together.

Chapter 36

2015

Friday night

Roger called me.

It was Friday night and I was still at work.

"Come home, we're going to a concert."

"You're kidding, really, where?"

"In New Brunswick."

"You realize I'm coming from New Jersey to go back to New Jersey?"

"Just come home."

"Honey, wouldn't you like to just veg tonight?" I said.

"Yes, but we're going."

"It's quite a drive," I said.

"You know what my father always said – "You can't go to too many parties in your life."

"I know, okay."

We left Brooklyn and made our way to New Brunswick. We found a perfect parking facility across the street from the theatre.

We texted our friend who had invited us, Gary, and he appeared magically in the main lobby of the theatre.

"Come here," he said.

He opened a very nondescript door and ushered us into a

beautiful, spacious, VIP bar area.

"Drinks are open."

Roger smiled. I knew this smile.

We had two rounds of beers and then made our way to the auditorium, bringing a third round with us.

Gary and his guests were up on the balcony. Roger and I were on the main floor.

The band began. We stood up in our seats and danced and clapped to the music. Lights surrounded us, and Roger held his hand on my back, bringing my shirt up, which drove me crazy. The energy coming off of him was astounding as he was rubbing my back. I turned and kissed him. His eyes were enormous, there was a white aura surrounding him as he looked at me – singing the words to the song. We stayed like that for the whole concert, loving every minute of the performance.

We left the concert taking pictures outside with Gary, his girlfriend and her friends to post on Facebook.

Little did I know these were the last pictures of Roger that I would ever see.

We drove home through Jersey, stopping at The Black Castle. Roger and I loved Black Castle and we ate sliders with veggie sliders with soda and fries.

Chapter 37
2015

Pity in my soul

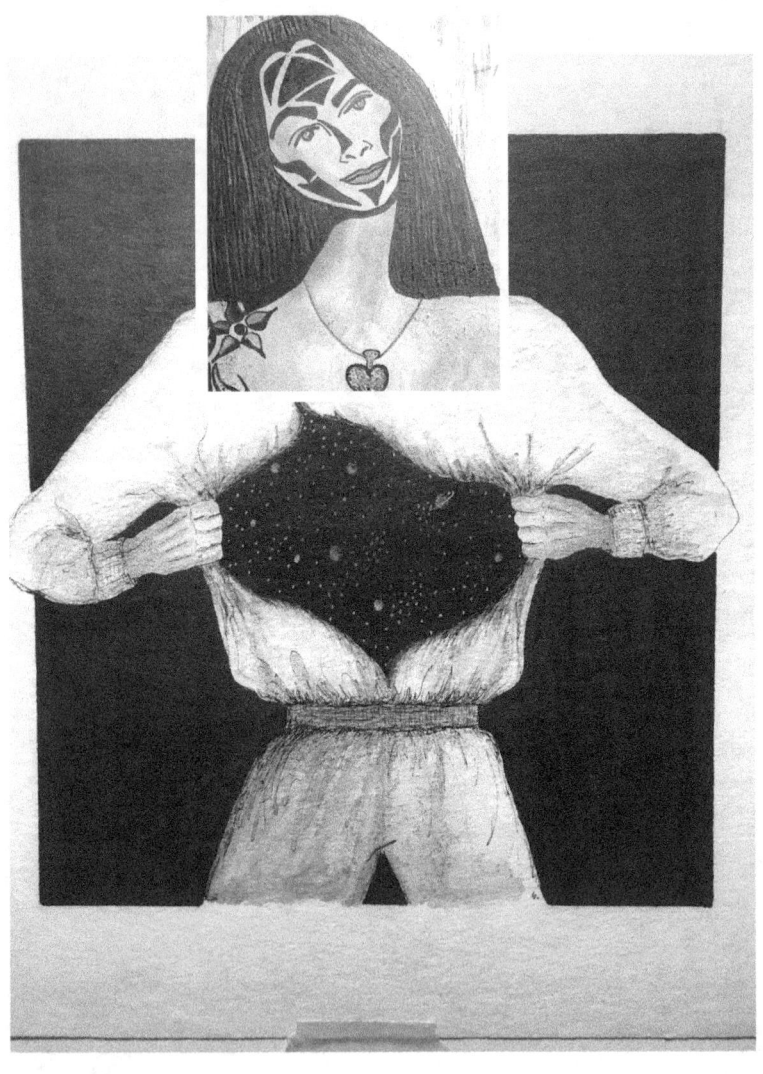

The next morning, Roger had promised his friend Brian to help him move. The plan was for him to get there, just around the corner, early, but Brian didn't call early so Roger slept late. Ten o'clock he got up and got dressed to go over to Brian's. He was wearing his father's necklace and I told him maybe he should not wear it – it might get ruined, but he did not listen to me. I was planning to get a haircut and then meet my mother. He left the house.

Ten minutes later Brian banged on my door.

"Cass, open up! It's Brian."

I opened the door.

"Get your bag, your ID, come with me, Roger has collapsed."

I grabbed my bag and followed him into the elevator. I could FEEL my gray streak coming in.

"What happened?" I frantically asked him.

"He collapsed," was all he would say.

When the elevator door opened we ran into the street and ran down the block turned the corner and ran into his house.

Roger was lying on the floor with the paramedics performing CPR on him. His chest was bare, they had a plastic mouthpiece over his mouth and nose and I nearly collapsed. They took me away from him and kept saying that they were working on him. I was hysterical, calling Olivia, my mother, and Beth. Many firemen and paramedics kept telling me that they were working on him, but I believed them.

They took him in an ambulance to the hospital and I followed in another ambulance. They took him to the emergency area and continued to work on him. I could see various nurses performing CPR, throwing their hands up and switching positions as I lost my mind.

Finally, the doctor on call ushered me into a private room with Brian and told me that he had passed. That he had a cardiac arrest. I screamed, I howled, I kicked, I shouted, I cried, I prayed, I didn't know what to do. My Roger was gone? My Roger was dead? I could not take this, this was not real. My Olivia came, my Beth came and then my Andy came. And they allowed me to see him.

I touched his face and it made me feel better. I felt his hair and it made me feel whole. I leaned over and kissed his cheek and it made me long for him all the more. I reached for his father's necklace and lifted it above his head, holding the heavy gold, still warm from his body. I couldn't breathe. I couldn't think. I couldn't believe what I was seeing, my Roger, my beautiful husband, my vivacious man, this was not him. Please God, wake him up, I cried. I believe in you God, please wake him up.

The nurses looked at me with pity in their eyes and I felt pity in my soul. He was so young, so special. He was gone.

His funeral was enormous, friends upon friends and family gathered to say goodbye to my Roger. His mother, my mother, and his sister Michelle sat there in shock. He would have been happy to see the crowd but sorry that he had missed the gathering.

The Friday after his funeral I found myself in the kitchen wondering how Roger was. I was sure he was in heaven performing rock concerts for the angels and having a grand old time. I walked over to his acoustic guitar and to my amazement the guitar moved and changed position. He was here, with me, I knew in my heart. I was not scared to see this but happy and comforted and I bent down and kissed the guitar. I told no one.

It was a sign.

Two weeks later on Roger's birthday I went back to work, not being able to concentrate or think clearly but trying to keep busy to keep my mind off of what had happened. I drove home from work, waiting at the timed red light on Rte. 1, my thoughts on Roger. A large truck was waiting for the light perpendicular to me. I saw a bright bright bright source of light and energy dancing off the front of the truck for what seemed like minutes and minutes. I tried to see where it may be coming from and if any other drivers saw this, but no, it was a show for only me. I told no one.

It was a sign.

I had a lonely lunch on the following Saturday at a neighborhood diner. I walked to the cashier to pay and stood for a moment at the front of the restaurant. An old woman with long gray hair in pigtails approached me. She was my height and stood in front of me.

"Look me in the eye."

I did.

"My eye is corrupted," she said.

Are you okay? she said.

"Are you alright?" she said.

"Are, Are, R, R, R, R, R," she said.

Roger was telling me something.

"I love you, love you, love you, take care of yourself," she said.

And she walked out of the restaurant.

I told no one.

It was a sign.

So many signs.

Nine PM. Time to take a walk.

I looked to the sky as I did every night these days to search for the star that reminded me of Roger. This star moved it's position slowly each night from the east toward the south. Speaking aloud, I told Roger that I hadn't seen him in the star for a few days as the last week had been overcast and the sky had been filled with clouds, fog.

As I turned to return home I looked down to find a beautiful present that had not been there before. A flower. Not like any of the flowers in the garden in front of the building but a unique flower open to the sky filled with raindrops and a stem curved, facing up above.

I looked at this token, this amazing gift that I knew Roger had sent to me. Afraid to touch it because it might disappear, I picked it up gently and kissed it. Looking up I thanked Roger for it and smiled. I was sure he was here with me and around me.

Around me, and around me, and around me, all around me he was.

Chapter 38
2015

I'm a rock star

One Sunday afternoon I sat on the couch and had a beer.

And then another one.

And then three more.

The TV was on, but I had no interest in it.

I reached for the *GQ Magazine* that our neighbor had left in front of our door weeks ago that Roger liked.

I opened the magazine and the images and words swirled into a circle and I saw Roger's face.

"Roger."

Text moved into a sentence.

Yes, honey, it's me.

"Oh, my, I miss you so much."

The letters moved again.

I know, Cass, I miss you too.

"Are you okay?"

The text swirled.

I'm okay, I'm a rock star here where I am. I have my family that have passed. David Bowie joins me for dinner and George Michael comes for poker. Even Fred the fish is here. Heaven is real. All of my dreams have come true except for having you with me.

"I don't know what to say, you left me too young."

Time will tell. I'll be here for you when your time comes. You're my best friend and my soul mate, always remember that. Don't worry about me. Live your life to the fullest, be happy, I love you dearly.

The magazine fell out of my hands.

Monday morning, 4:45 am, much too early. Tossing my slumber aside I climbed out of bed as I had promised my neighbor a ride to the airport.

I rang Joe's bell at 5:30.

"Ready?" I asked as he opened the door, his suitcase in hand.

"Couldn't be more ready for Florida!" he laughed.

We chatted on the way to JFK. Gossip about the neighbors, his anticipation of seeing his Florida friends, his longing to see his sister. He kept me awake and occupied with his talking. I was still tired and driving on auto pilot listening to the sound of his voice.

"Cass, you know if you ever need anything I'm here for you," he said looking at me. My eyes never left the road. "Unless of course if I'm in Florida." We laughed together.

"Thank you, Joe, you know I love you!"

I dropped him at the Jet Blue terminal waving as he approached the curbside check in.

I made my way out of the JFK compound back onto the Belt Parkway, west towards the Verrazzano Bridge. I might as well get to the office early and lay down for a nap, I thought. Better than going home and starting all over again.

Traffic.

Stop.

Go.

Stop.

Go a little more.

Rocking me back and forth.

Twenty minutes on the highway at least until a chance to get some coffee.

Stop.

Go.

Fifteen minutes.

Traffic.

Stop.

Go.

Ten minutes.

I couldn't keep my eyes open.

They kept closing.

If only I could close my eyes for a minute, I kept thinking.

Five minutes. I can do this.

Traffic.

Stop.

Go.

Rocking back and forth.

I put the radio on.

LOUD, and then LOUDER.

I opened the windows to let the air in but the air was warm and not refreshing.

I screamed and sang and screamed again and thought that I was okay.

If only I could close my eyes for a minute. I kept thinking.

I missed my exit for coffee and started to follow the lane to the incline to the bridge.

My head rolled. My eyes could not stay open.

The exhausted feeling in my eyes was overtaking my whole

being, until I hit the car in the next lane.

THEN– I was fully awake.

Oh, no, I hit a car.

Oh, SHIT, I hit a car.

FUCK FUCK FUCK I HIT THE CAR IN THE NEXT LANE.

I WAS REALLY FULLY AWAKE NOW.

I never felt so certain that a car was a weapon until I hit this car.

The driver side mirror flew off the brand new white Mercedes next to me.

I had crashed into the front drivers side panel of the pristine new car, hard.

The female driver looked at me.

I opened my passenger window to begin the lament of what I had done. The lies came to me quickly and naturally. I was changing my glasses. I didn't see her. It wasn't my fault. I was an evil child lying through my teeth.

She opened her window and said "Let's drive to the other side of the bridge so not to block traffic – follow me."

And I did. I followed her over the bridge cursing myself for my stupidity. For my lack of control. For what may come. We crossed the bridge and she pulled over to the right lane where the Troopers were. They surrounded us like vultures on a carcass, waiting to feed.

I got out of my car. They told me to get back in. I looked at the female driver and as she looked at me she screamed.

"I KNOW YOU," she cried, pointing at me with her finger while holding onto her steering wheel, her freshly polished white nails groping the wheel and her long dark hair blowing wildly from the open window.

"I'VE SEEN YOU BEFORE."

It was her, Marissa Ringel. The poetess from so many years ago at the club in the Village – from so long ago.

She recognized me and I recognized her.

"YOU BITCH! YOUR DIDN'T LISTEN TO ME THEN. GO BACK, GO BACK, GO BACK WHERE YOU CAME FROM, HE'S STILL FUCKEN WAITING —I TOLD YOU THEN AND I TELL YOU NOW!"

————"I TOLD YOU– AND NOW LOOK WHAT YOU'VE DONE............."

And then the time passed.

And I mourned him, and our friends mourned him.

His dear friend Billy had written a poem for Roger and had presented it to me in a beautiful frame. Laura had created a slide show of pictures of Roger and all his friends.

I counted the weeks, one by one that he was gone.

Well-meaning people asked how I was.

"I'm hanging in."

"I'm taking it one day at a time."

"I have my moments."

"I have my meltdowns."

"I know he's gone to heaven and is in a better place."

"I'm doing alright...."

And I missed him so much.

And I was alone.

I looked in the nooks and crannies of our apartment, delving into old notebooks and found writings of Roger that seemed to be so true now and that comforted me.

Shoot you a sign
Won't see you tomorrow
Though I'm not here now
Forget the sorrow
We gave it all that we had to give
And what's done is done
Now it's time to live
But every now and then
If you stare at the stars
I'll shoot you a sign from heaven
Yeah shoot you a sign
And when the night falls
I look over you
You take a picture and I'm your flash cube
I'll shoot you a sign from heaven
Shoot you a sign

I went to work each day pretending to be okay, smiling at the picture of Roger on my desk.

I came home each night to speak to the photo I had hung in my kitchen of Roger.

We laughed together, we cried together, me and the photo. I even managed to cook one night, gazing into his denim blue eyes, his handsome face. That night I fell asleep early, wanting to avoid the long lonely evening. My sleep was speckled with dreams. Roger walking down the block toward me. Roger laughing and smiling.

Roger spending time in the mirror grooming, Roger driving with Steele Blonde playing.

I drove home one day; the rain was pouring down. I found myself driving to Roger's old friend Ronnie's house nearby. I stopped the car and called Ronnie.

"Are you home? Can you step out? I'm in front of your house."

I sat in the car until he emerged with an umbrella in a white t-shirt. I got out of the car.

"I MISS HIM!" I screamed, tears running down my face as the rain ran down from the sky.

"I needed to see you," I said.

"Cassidy, I know, please, you're making me cry."

"I MISS HIM," I screamed again, looking about.

The rain was coming down in buckets, matching the horror in my soul.

I hugged Ronnie and returned to my car.

I went home and wept and slept.

And then HE appeared in my dreams. HE stood in front of HIS hearth, arms spread on the mantle. HE was angry.

"I am tired of this nonsensical behavior, this DEAL, these RULES. I WANT YOU BACK WHERE YOU BELONG."

The marble mantle shivered and cracked and came apart in pieces at his touch.

"I FEEL YOUR HEART AND I FEEL IT BREAKING. Human life is NOT WORTH THIS. BE QUICK ABOUT GETTING HOME FOR I WILL NOT WAIT FOREVER REGARDLESS OF OUR DEAL."

I moved in my sleep, feeling uncomfortable, and turned over onto my side into a dark, deep, slumber.

And then, one Saturday.
Thoughts were coming rapidly too many to focus.

I took my pills
and I took my pills
and I took my pills
and I took my pills
way too much
....Too much was never enough
and I took them again and again and again
but I took them again and again and again
Thoughts were
I took them again and again and again
Coming slowly
but I took them again and again and again
Too slowly to focus

I laid down on the couch with a terrible feeling
My mother, Olivia, Amber, I missed them already

I fell into a deep sleep.

Roger was calling to me – Cassidy!

HE was in his chamber, sitting on his throne. HE was there, beckoning to me – Come to me, Cassendre. How many times must I let you know. How much can I long for you? The butterfly beats his wings for too long. I HAVE HAD ENOUGH OF THIS. I am tired of waiting for you, time is of the essence, I can't see how much longer I can wait for you and these rules to end.

My heart was failing
Beating
So slowly
My life essence was draining
The pills were taking their effect
I was dying
Roger was waiting
HE was waiting
I felt my life spirit draining out
Happily, I was dying
My life, my two lives were fighting and all I wanted to do was to let go.
I breathed slowly
and then more slowly
My last breaths brought familiar words:
One's life flashes forward on the moment before death, showing where one's soul energy will go when death is finally upon them.

"MASTER COME!" Vincent burst into HIS Chambers.
"What is it, Vincent?"

THE CASSENDRE DECREE

"COME, CASSENDRE IS DYING!"
HE touched Vincent's arm and they appeared in The Moderation Rooms.
"LOCK INTO CASSENDRE," HE screamed to the operator.

The operator opened up the virtual spectator, hands shaking.
They saw her laying on the couch.
Her thoughts flashed across the screen:

I'm not sorry for all I've done.
I have felt, accomplished, cultivated, and experienced
    a true human existence.

My time as a human has made me a better soul.

I have learned so much and have loved so much
on this earthly plane.
My dear husband has died and I can hear his words:
Close your eyes and see
Don't breathe so hard
and catch your breath
Slow down some
and smell the flowers
In time
The years will seem like hours

Rog –
The time went by
A whisper
A sound

THE CASSENDRE DECREE

A glance at your picture
Missing you fiercely
Still
Thunderstorms
– just not the same
My love
I see you in the star
On the Northern sky
Every night
The piece inside of me
That only you fit
You are missed so
And loved much
I can't believe you're gone
I drive, and I search for songs on the radio
        that remind me of you
I miss you more than words can say

DON'T Rest in Peace, my love –

ROCK ON IN HEAVEN!

Heaven is real, I believe, and I know I will see you again

Be well, be strong, and know
that you are always in my thoughts and in my heart
I alone am the keeper of your memories–
Not of your memory– family and friends keep you close–
But I keep the intimate knowledge of the life you led
the things that truly made you Roger

THE CASSENDRE DECREE

The music that you played in the soft moments after midnight
The movies that you loved so much
that you watched them more than twice
The rainy days we spent loving the thunder
and the nights when we watched the sun rise
The sad times and the silly times and the day-to-day living
I will love you forever
It's been a surreal time
Forever long, counting each moment that you've been gone
Yet time flows by in an instant
For it feels like yesterday that you were here beside me
I miss you beyond any words I can say
I love you Roger—

You will always be in my heart
————Tears.
When all the words in your heart can't make a proper sentence
It's the one tear that falls to earth that made life worthwhile.

My MAN that has allowed my dreams to come true is waiting.

I only regret not having seen more of this beautiful earth
nor having had brought a child into it

oh
my
I find difficulty in breathing
The pills I have taken leave me breathless
oh
oh

HE and Vincent watched in awe as she spoke
I
I
I love...

She expired upon those words.
HE looked to Vincent.
HE looked to the screen hoping, praying if HE could use the term, with every cell in HIS being to see that her soul energy would come back to HIM.
To HIS horror HE saw that her soul energy was drifting upward, like a beautiful flower of spirit ascending upward and HE cried out.
————————"NOOOOOOOOOOOOOOOO."

Chapter 39

Now

Is here heaven?

She floated.
On a sea of grey clouds – for a moment.
For a moment.
The grey clouds opened for a tiny ray of sunlight to entertain the
thought of slipping through.
And.
Then it did.
It came.
It came through and took over the space that she was in.
The all encompassing space.
That she was in.
From the North, the South, the 1,2,3,4
The all over and over of the bright light.

She whispered to herself.
She shouted to herself.
She screamed just because
it felt so right
so becoming and so birthing.
She stood up and took a tentative step
just in front.

"I have no right to be here"
"WHERE IS HERE?
It is white here
is here heaven?"
The skies turned black.
A vacuum but she could still see her hands.
"It is black here
is here heaven?"

She pushed off of her toes with a jump and floated into the
blackness above her.
The blackness opened for a tiny ray of sunlight.
It did.
It came.
It came through and took over the space that she was in.
The all encompassing space.
That she was in.

She looked around at the bright bright emptiness.
I don't belong here, she thought.
There are no marching bands welcoming me with open arms.
Nor
Is my lover here to greet me.

The clouds gathered at her feet as she began to move in a circle.
"Where are YOU!"
She screamed to the emptiness.
"What nonsense is this?"
She turned in a circle in the emptiness.
"SOMETHING IS VERY WRONG!"

She took a long, deep breath and walked forward into the mist.
So, here I am.
I am alone.
Is this what I've always thought would be?
How fucken interesting!
Is it simply ME, ME, ME FOR ETERNITY?
Ha!
She laughed out loud to herself.
Is this really how it ends?

Suddenly–
HE appeared.
HE appeared in front of her rising from the clouds.
HIS hand was outstretched, HIS smile very wide and absolutely wicked.

"My love. This is how it begins."

The Rules

Rules

She must agree to live as a normal human—
with issues and/or full of happiness and/or sorrow

She must agree to be checked in upon—
Vincent, dreams, intermittent spiritual visits from HIM

She must agree not to be religious

She must agree that time may be subjective

She must agree to a control factor—
illness/pills and manage it
(This was her deal breaker but she declared,
"I will overcome this.")

HE must agree to only hear her not "see" her in real time—
(This was HIS deal breaker but HE declared
"I will overcome this.")

HE must agree to be able to contact her only via thoughts/
dreams/spirituality

HE MUST AGREE TO WAIT FOR HER DEATH
BEFORE SHE WILL RETURN

Sheryl Lynn Rosenstock Marcus
lives in Brooklyn, NY.

Sheryl is a partner in a creative design studio;
an artist of paint, multimedia, craft and words.

This is her first novel.

Photo Credit: Shunsuke Takino